Hiding Abigail

The girl with the Yellow Star

Brendan Mac an Mhaoir

Hiding Abigail. The Girl with the Yellow Star

Introduction

My father was born in the 1930's. It was during the 1940's when he sat in class beside a German boy named Deiter.

Deiter was a long way from home and the war had not long ended, both boys had one thing in common, they were both very poor.

They sat together with nothing to share but their stories.

Hiding Abigail. The Girl with the Yellow Star

Chapter One

February 2nd 1942

Day eight

Waking up in the countryside

I could feel myself slowly waking up, you know that moment when you realise the dream you're dreaming isn't actually real but as you wake you think, no please don't wake, not yet, like you don't want to go back to the real world but just stay in your dream. I opened my eyes and looked at the strange ceiling in this bedroom. I lay there for a minute thinking about the dream I had just finished or rather not finished. I was thinking to myself should I try to go back asleep and finish my dream, but now a minute later I had forgotten what I was even dreaming about.

I noticed everything was different, I noticed the silence. I noticed this room was not my bedroom and then everything came flooding back into my head, everything that had happened over the past week, the past seven days to be exact.

Abigail and the secret door, the burning of the books, the Soldiers, the dogs, the animal trains, the planes, the rumbling like thunder and the flashing lights coming out of the ground, the red flags and the yellow stars, the great speech, the buildings chopped in half, the blond soldier in the black uniform, the singing on the trams and sleighing in the snow down the hill beside the train as we travelled home. All of this flashing back into my head at once as if it was one big nightmare that had happened over the past number of months or maybe years. But everything that was flooding now back into my memories actually happened in the last seven days.

I jumped out of bed faster than I have ever done so before and ran straight to the bedroom window to see where I was. The glass was frozen over on the inside. I made a fist shape with my right hand and with the side of my fist I started rubbing the glass to try to defrost at least the smallest section of glass so as I could see where I was and what this place looked like, was there anybody else here and was there going to be even anything to do. As usual like at home it only took about one minute to defrost a little piece of glass, just enough for me to see out.

I looked out and for a moment I couldn't believe my eyes. There was nothing. No houses or no people, No streets or no shops, no buildings, red flags, soldiers, cars or trams. No movement what so ever. Only fields and trees as far as the eye could see. A wire fence about twenty steps away and large mountains in the distance and everything covered in a blanket of snow. I stood for a few minutes looking out the window at the snow gently falling which as always was helping me to go into a kind of daydream or it was as if the snow falling was hypnotising me.

I thought back over the previous seven days and everything that had happened and how everything in my life had changed so much in such a short space of time. I thought about how in only seven days the whole world had changed. I thought about Abigail and I thought back to where it had all began. It was that day in school where all these changes started. The day was much the same as today with me looking out the window at the snow falling, and in a daydream.

Chapter Two
January 26th 1942
Day One
The burning of the books

I sat in class and I just couldn't wait for the school day to end, I sat in my seat with my elbow on the table and my hand on my cheek holding up my head. Every so often I would fall asleep and my head would fall forward and out of my hand and just before it would hit the table I would wake up again and sit back up as straight as possible before anyone would notice.

The teacher stood at the front of the class rambling on about I'm not sure what, but usually it was the war, the first war that is and I'd heard it so many times before from my teacher, Grandmother and most old people you met these days. All old people spoke about was the war or how hard things were when they were young or about when they went to school and how cold it was back then.

I sat in class beside Siegfried Schulte most days now and teacher said I was to help him with his work. Siegfried was two years older than me and also two years older than everyone in our class. He wasn't always in our class but he was this year.

8

It's not that he wasn't always in our school but just not always in our class. Last year he was one class ahead of me and the year before as far as I can remember he was two classes ahead. But for this year he was in our class. Teacher gave Siegfried the job of ringing the bell at the end of school every day and he seemed to really enjoy doing it and claimed that he was the only one in the whole school capable of doing such an important job. He had what everybody called red hair but it wasn't really red like the flags in our town but more the colour of rust or maybe the leaves in autumn.

Siegfried had beaten me in a sports day race once and he'd gotten the gold medal and I the silver medal. I can't remember who got the bronze medal because I suppose I never noticed who was running behind me. But I do know that everyone in our race was my age except Siegfried and I don't think he was supposed to be there. I can remember clearly that Mother wasn't happy about it and thought I should have gotten the gold but I didn't really mind because most of the boys got no medal at all.

Siegfried was always asking the teacher a question about something from when they were young or a question about the war. He wasn't really interested all he wanted to do was to get him to talk about the old days and for the teacher to get lost in the story and just ramble on while the class sat back and did nothing, maybe that's why Siegfried has stayed back twice now. He was always doing this and we all knew it and today that's exactly what was happening.

I sat looking out the window at the snow gently falling on the trees outside, which was only helping to put me to sleep when I noticed there was Father standing at the School gate as he has done every day for as long as I can remember, waiting for my brother and I to come running out of class. Mother used to say 'With That infectious Smile on his face.' Now I don't really know what the word Infectious means but surely it has to be something good. It sounds a lot like the word infection to me, which is something I once got on my toe, when my toenail grew in the wrong direction and that really wasn't very nice at all.

Mother and Father always used words that children just didn't understand but that was fine because we understood most of what they were saying. Collecting us from school I think was my Fathers favourite part of his day, not only because he was there with his two sons that he said he loved more than anything in the world but he was also getting out of his shop for one hour, for a walk and some fresh air. Every day he hugged us both at the School gate, me first because I always got to the gate first, because I was faster and my little brother second. This was to be our last day of School for a long time but we just didn't know it yet.

Now when I say my little brother I actually mean my younger brother, because much to my embarrassment my younger brother Hans was taller than me. Now it wasn't very noticeable because whenever we did stand side by side and anybody was looking I would get up on my tippy toes ever so slightly. Hans knew I was doing this but he didn't mind because I noticed sometimes he would bend his knees or roll his shoulders forward and downwards ever so slightly at the same time to make himself look smaller. We didn't plan this or we never spoke of it, it just happened, an unconscious reaction or an agreement of sorts between two brothers. Most people mistook us for twins even though my brother had blond hair and I had brown hair. Now I didn't mind people thinking we were twins because it saved me explaining that I was older, one year and two months older and on the day of my birthday and for two months after I was two years older and two inches smaller. Next birthday I would be eleven years old and Hans would be still only nine.

Every day we would take that long walk home from School back to our house which was also a little book shop on Bilker Street. Now on this day which I will never forget it was extra cold. The snow was falling and blowing into our faces as we walked up through the long narrow cobble stone streets with the tram lines hidden this time of year by the snow, towards the Square in the centre of town.

It was starting to get dark. It always seemed to be dark or nearly dark. Everywhere and everything in our town just seemed to be grey and colourless. Recently the world just looked like a blur of grey and white with dots of red. Those dots of red being those flags that hung from every house and shop in town. Red flags with a white circle and a strange black sign in the centre. We had one hanging outside our house just between my bedroom window and Mother and Father's bedroom. When I looked out my window I could see our flag and I could see everyone on our street had their flag out, everyone except for one house which was straight across the street from ours. As we got near the end of Grabbepl Street just before we turned left into the town square I looked across at Hans who was on my Fathers left, for some reason Hans always held my Fathers left hand and I his right. I noticed Hans was walking with his eyes closed, his red face looking upwards and his mouth open, his tongue sticking out like my Father was checking to see if it was black, because everybody knew if you told a lie your tongue turned black. But on this occasion nobody was checking his tongue, Hans was actually catching Snowflakes. What a brilliant idea and why hadn't I thought of it.

Too busy daydreaming, too busy looking at those silly flags and trying to figure them out, too busy listening to the snow crunching under our feet, too busy thinking about Abigail Blaustein in her red dress, the girl from the house across the street from ours that had no red flag but who along with those flags was the only other bit of colour in this world. The girl from the house across the street who didn't go to our school or never spoke to me. But then I suppose I never spoke to her either, mainly because every time I passed her in the street I froze and went into some sort of shock with a tingling pain in my chest.

Catching Snowflakes on one's tongue now this was something I just had to try. So before we turned left into the town square I looked upwards, closed my eyes, opened my mouth and stuck my tongue out as far as it would go. My cheeks were stinging with the cold, my lips were sore and probably blue by now, but my tongue for the moment was warm and just perfect for catching snowflakes. I could feel the flakes land on my tongue and melt, the taste was not strong but was just fresher than you could ever imagine or fresher than anything I have ever tasted. We turned the corner into the Square and with my eyes still closed, mouth still open, tongue still out and feeling that there was no need to see where we were going as Father and his warm hands would keep us on the right path.

Then something changed, the snow was no longer melting on my tongue and it didn't taste the same anymore either, even with my eyes closed I could see a bright light flickering in the distance through my eyelids. I opened my eyes at once and looked across at Hans who was looking back at me. There were black flakes on his face and probably on mine too. We both looked up at Father and then up to the Sky. The snow had turned black and was falling straight down on top of us.

Father started moving much faster now across the snowy cobble stones through the Square. Towards the top of the Square where there was a large building called The Town Hall which had a clock tower. The Town Hall was covered in those red flags which were larger than most of the flags in town. Outside The Town Hall was a large Bronze Statue of a Horse with a man on his back, a man with long hair and a silly hat. A large crowd had gathered close to the statue in the middle of the square. When we got to the front of the crowd it was only then that Hans and I could now see what was happening.

A huge fire had been built close to the middle of the Square, a huge fire of nothing only books. I looked up at my Father who had a look of shock on his face and then across at Hans who just looked very confused. I've seen this look on their faces before so I knew I was right. I've seen every look on my Father's face, anger, sadness, happiness, confusion and tonight it was shock but never have I seen it expressed in this way or so strongly before tonight. That black snow that landed on our faces was actually ash and it wasn't landing on top of us anymore but rather floating now up into the night air and over our heads and was blowing towards the lower end of the Square where we had just come from. More books were now being thrown on the fire by the Soldiers, the soldiers that always wore those really smart uniforms and by the large crowds that had gathered. I don't know what Father or Hans were thinking but I stood there with my cheeks now burning from the heat of the fire thinking to myself that if they didn't want these books anymore we could have sold them in our book shop or if they were damaged Father could have fixed them up like new because in the last year or so Father hasn't been very busy fixing books or selling books. Mother says 'Nobody has any money these days' I also thought to myself if nobody wants these books anymore and they're only fit for burning we could have burned them in our fire place in the shop and kept the shop and the house really warm. I stood there thinking to myself what a waste of heat and what a waste of books. But at least for now I felt really warm again while we stood outside in the town square near the clock tower and the statue of the horse with the man on his back on that cold snowy night trying to figure it all out.

Everything seemed to fall silent but for the sound of the fire. Then all at once everybody started to sing, gently at first. I looked up at my Father who was such a tall man, the tallest amongst all his friends and I could see the tears were coming from his eyes and turning red from the glow of the fire as they ran down his cheeks, and stopped at his lips for a split second then moved slowly to his chin before they fell off onto the lapel of his Jacket.

Everybody sang together. I wasn't really sure what the words of the song were so I couldn't really join in and even if I did know what the words were I wouldn't join in anyway because I wasn't really much of a singer. In fact I was a terrible singer and when we sang in school I was afraid to join in just in case if everyone stopped at the same time I'd be left singing on my own. My Grandfather was a great singer and I'd sang a song for him once and then asked if he thought I could sing. He said I could sing alright and that I should always sing but just not to do it in public. I'd heard this song before because we sang it in school sometimes in the morning and I remember it best from when I had heard it sang when I was eight over two years ago when my two older brothers Edward and Gustav had joined the Army. Edward was twelve years older than me and Gustav nine. I hadn't seen Edward or Gustav since they had left, and we didn't know where they were anymore. The only news we had heard of Edward or Gustav was that Edward had won a medal in his first year in the army but we have never seen it or we're not exactly sure what he won it for. Maybe he won it in a race like when I won a silver medal the day Siegfried got the gold medal which Mother still wasn't very happy about.

Well I'm not sure if it was a medal that Edward won but from what I remember hearing at the time, it was more of an iron cross than a medal. I really missed them both but they had to go.

Father, Mother, Hans or I didn't want them to go away but it seems we need lots of Soldiers in smart uniforms if we are to make our Country great again.

Chapter Three

January 27th 1942

Day Two

Everything is changing

Early the next morning I was awoken by the sound of my Mother's voice. Mother was standing at the bottom of the stairs calling us both to get up. I hated getting up early on these cold mornings. Most mornings I would get dressed under the blankets before I would dare get out of the bed. Once more Mother shouted from the bottom of the stairs.

'Hans.'

'Deiter.'

'Get up at once. I have something to talk to you about.' Oh no! I thought to myself. There were so many thoughts dancing through my mind when I heard the line 'I have something to talk to you about,' and I was trying to remember what Hans or I had gotten up to in the previous week. But I couldn't think of anything only maybe that the evening before Hans and I had held our arms up in the air just like everybody else, while they were singing that song. That strange salute that everybody had to do these days that Mother and Father hated doing and avoided. I didn't much care for it either because it only made my arm tired. But I have a feeling that wasn't it because there was no mention of it last night when we got home.

I jumped out of bed already dressed and ran straight to the window in my room to see what was happening on the street below. For a long time now all that I've noticed out of my window were soldiers marching in their smart uniforms like what Edward and Gustav were wearing the last time I had seen them. But in the last week or so I had noticed less and less Soldiers on the streets. I also had noticed that at night there was the sound of more and more planes in the sky. And this was the reason why we had to keep the lights off at night and the curtains closed because those men in the planes might see us.

As I tried to look out my window I noticed that as usual the inside of the window which faced to the front of the house and onto the street was frozen and I couldn't see out. It was a small Dormer window with not much glass in it and I started to rub it with the side of my fist in circles to try get rid of the frost until after around one minute I could see out. I had a perfect little circle of clear glass to see the world, the weather and the people below slowly making their way up and down the snowy slippery footpaths.

Then my heart sort of skipped a beat. I could see Abigail Blaustein playing with one of her friends on the street across from our house. I don't know her friends name or any of her friends names for that matter. I just know Abigail Blaustein's name. She had dark brown hair even darker than mine and she was wearing her red dress and a dark coloured coat with a patch on the front in the shape of a yellow star. A lot of people in our town were wearing those yellow stars on their coats but I'm not really sure why and Mother nor Father would explain to me why this was any time I asked. So I just gave up asking.

Maybe today would be the day I might find the courage to talk to or even say hello to Abigail Blaustein. But it's all very well saying hello. The problem is not saying hello but trying to think what could I say next? What would we talk about? If I could even talk because knowing me I would probably just freeze on the spot or start stammering like I sometimes do when I'm in school when teacher asks me a question that I don't know or sometimes a question that I do know the answer to and I just stammer anyway. What would Abigail Blaustein think of me if I just stood in front of her shaking and stammering and not able to talk or even say a single word. I don't think Abigail Blaustein would ever want to talk to me again.

Maybe I could just say hello and ask her a short question, and let her do all the talking. Maybe I could ask her a question about school or the yellow star on her coat. That's two questions and that would probably be enough to keep her talking for long enough while I recover from the shock and get my breathing back to normal. When my breathing is normal I can talk to people no problem at all. I can have a perfect conversation with anybody but just don't ask me a question out of the blue even if I know the answer because that's where I get stuck very fast and start to stammer.

While I stood there looking down at Abigail Blaustein on the street below through my little dormer window and thinking about what I would say to her I noticed she was looking back at me. My heart nearly stopped. I jumped back at once before she could see me, but it was too late. She had seen me staring at her with more than likely a silly expression on my face and probably talking to myself while wiping snot that ran from my nose or with a silly smile. I don't know what I must have looked like staring out that window but I know it couldn't be good.

Now before I had any time to worry myself any further about this, I heard Mother again at the bottom of the stairs calling for Hans and I to come downstairs at once. She had something very important to talk to us about. Now I had something else to worry about and the staring at Abigail Blaustein was very quickly forgotten. What had Mother to talk to us about or what had Hans or I done wrong of late that she was only finding out about this morning.

I tip toed out of my room and into my brother Hans bedroom which was at the back of the house and faced the back garden. Hans also had a small bedroom like mine with a small dormer window. Our bedrooms were small but at least we had a bedroom all to ourselves which wasn't always the case. Edward and Gustav used to share the front room and Hans and I the back bedroom. When Edward and Gustav left to join the army I moved to the front bedroom which had its advantages. The view was so much better.

The view from the back bedroom was fine but all there was to see was the back garden which was very small. And other peoples back gardens, a few trees and lots of little sheds and in our garden a white coloured sink with flowers but mostly weeds growing in it and a stack of old cobble stones. A few old galvanised buckets and an old kennel that wasn't used anymore and lots of old bicycles and other silly old stuff which was boring and not really worth looking at.

The view from my room was so much better, so much more interesting. You could see the red flags and the soldiers marching, you could see if a car drove past which didn't happen very often but if it did you could see what it looked like or who was driving it. You could see who was going into the shop and most importantly you could see Abigail Blaustein playing with her friends. You could sit all day if you wanted and watch the people go up and down the street doing what they had to do. Sounds boring but for me it was actually interesting for some reason and a great way to pass time on these boring winter days. The only advantage Hans bedroom had was you could climb out through his bedroom window and slide down a short distance onto a flat roof at the back of the house which was actually part of the kitchen roof.

Every winter the snow would build up really high on the flat roof and Father would have to climb out and sweep it away before it got too heavy and the roof might collapse and fall in on top of Mother in the kitchen. Nobody else was allowed climb out there only Father because this was another place in the house like the office that was off limits, off limits full stop as Mother used to say.

A few years ago when I was only maybe seven Gustav climbed out onto the flat roof and piled up all the snow on the roof and left it straight over the back door. Everybody was in on the plan except me, and everyone knew what was happening when Hans asked me to go outside with him and I did without hesitation. When we got just outside the back door he stopped and starting pointing up into a tree in the neighbours back garden and asked me if I could see the birds nest. I stood there and looked as carefully as I could and tried to focus in on different parts of the tree to see if I could see the nest but I couldn't see a thing. I stood there wishing I could see it because I loved to climb trees and find bird's nests. Hans walked away slowly and left me standing there on my own and as soon as he did Gustav swept every bit of snow that was piled up on the roof straight down on top of my head. So much snow that I ended up on my knees on the ground and Hans, Gustav, and Edward who had just arrived all had such a great laugh. Father was standing looking out through the kitchen window laughing and Mother walked out the back door past me and said with a big smile on her face.

'I thought you were a snowman.'
That was the type of thing that Gustav and Hans loved to do and they were always busy trying to fool somebody. For the rest of the winter everyone had such a laugh every time they talked about the day they swept the snow down on top of me and I ended up looking like a snowman.

Hans was still in bed when I tip toed in but I noticed like me he was getting dressed under the blankets. I said to Hans.

'Do you know what Mother wants to talk to us about?'

'No' Replied Hans.

'We haven't done anything recently that Mother is only finding out about now.' I asked.

'I don't think so.' Hans paused for a while and then smiled and said. 'I haven't skipped school in months.' Hans was always skipping school and the last time he skipped school he hid up a tree for the whole day. Coming near the end of the day and when he was getting really bored and hungry he saw somebody cycling past on their bicycle. Hans shouted down.

'Excuse me but would you have the time please?' Much to his surprise Father replied.

'It's three o clock Hans and time for you to go home from school now.' Father never ever told Mother.

Hans then looked at me and said. 'The last thing I remember us doing wrong was eating the bar of chocolate.' We both laughed.

You see a few years ago and before this silly war started, Father would sometimes bring chocolate home. We haven't seen chocolate now for a few years but when Father did bring it home there was great excitement. One evening Father brought home two large bars of chocolate which doubled the excitement because normally he would only bring one. We shared the first bar between the six of us, each getting three squares. I would eat my three squares of chocolate so carefully and as slow as I could, trying to make the beautiful sweet taste last longer. I'd never use my teeth when eating chocolate just my tongue. I would never bite the chocolate just break it into three separate squares, putting one square into my mouth at a time and then let it melt slowly. When we finished our chocolate on this night in question Father then said we would keep the other bar for tomorrow evening, which was fine with everybody.

Now Hans and I had a different idea. After dark when everybody had fallen asleep I tip toed down the stairs very slowly making sure to avoid the very bottom step of the stairs which always made a very annoying sound like chalk on a black board. The sound of the bottom step wasn't very noticeable during the day but at night when everybody was asleep and everything was quiet it was like a cat when you accidentally stepped on its tail.

I went into the shop through the secret door. I stole the bar of chocolate from Father's top drawer in his office. The same top drawer where he kept his gun that used to belong to Grandfather. I turned and headed back up the stairs with my heart pounding so loudly in my chest that I thought it would surely wake Mother or Father. When I got to the top of the stairs I met Edward who whispered.

'Where are you going?'

'Coming from the bathroom' I whispered in a shaky voice.

'Goodnight' he said very softly and went back into his room. I went back into mine where Hans and I sat on his bed for over an hour eating eighteen squares of chocolate between us. Now for some reason eating all those squares of chocolate although very nice wasn't as nice as those three squares of chocolate we had every month.

The next morning I was awoken by Mother Shouting at the top of her voice and pounding her way up the stairs screaming.

'WHO TOOK THE CHOCOLATE?!'

Oh no I thought to myself and I buried my head under the blankets and put the pillow over my head for protection. Our door swung open with an almighty crash against the wall behind it and the loud footsteps came across the room. I waited. I curled up into a ball. I held my breath. I pulled the pillow even tighter around my head. I knew what the pain that was about to hit me was like. I'd felt it before and I prepared myself for the worst. Then the sound of a large slap, but I felt nothing. Another slap and still I felt nothing. I was now guessing it was on the side of my brother's head as he let out an almighty scream. Two more slaps, maybe even three. I was losing count. My Mother was screaming but I don't know what she was saying. I peeped out from under the blankets and looked across at my brother's bed. Hans was crying, another slap, or two. Hans looked across at me waiting for me to say something but I stayed quiet. I felt it was the much safer thing to do. Mother then stormed out of the room and slammed the door behind her and banged her feet on every step as she went back down the stairs. Hans and I both sat up in our beds and looked at each other. We were both glad it was all over, Hans more so than I. It was then we noticed all the chocolate wrappers were left on his bed and there was a piece of melted chocolate near the top of one of his blankets where we had sat the night before. Hans looked at me with a look of a child recovering from shock and with the shape of a small red hand on his face, which looked extremely sore, tears on his cheeks and then a big smile came across his face and he said. 'Ah sure it was worth it' We both knew that chocolate was not our problem this morning and the only way we were going to find out, was to go downstairs and face up to it. I said to Hans. 'It couldn't be that bad otherwise Mother would have come up the stairs.' Hans got out of bed and we both walked together quietly down the stairs not knowing what was coming next. I was thinking back on the chocolate and feeling bad for Hans, and still at the back of my mind worrying about what Abigail Blaustein was thinking about me staring at her out through the window.

Hans and I walked into the Kitchen which faced towards the back of the house. We sat at the kitchen table which was over beside a window that was always steamed up and that looked out onto the back garden. Father was in the shop working. Mother was making breakfast and Hans and I sat at the table wondering what was happening. We sat there quietly for a while and as usual at any chance when I was feeling bored I would look out the window at the snow falling which was once again helping me to feel very relaxed and I started to daydream. Falling snow can have that effect on you sometimes. After a few minutes Father came into the kitchen and sat at the table. He looked like he was feeling sad and I thought to myself once again what could be wrong. I thought maybe Edward or Gustav had been hurt or maybe even shot while they were away at the War. Mother then turned to us and with a look of great sadness on her face she said.

'They are evacuating all the children from the city.' Now this was another one of those words that adults used that children just didn't understand. All I understood was something about all the children.

'What do you mean evac....' I'd forgotten the word already.

'What do you mean?' I said. Mother now looking out the window at the snow and with tears now coming from her eyes she said. 'All the women and children will have to leave the city. We are going to have to go away for a short while to the countryside but we will be home in around six months.' There was a long silence. There were so many questions in my head now that I couldn't think which ones to ask first.

'Is Father coming?' Father looked up at me and said.

'I'll be staying behind to mind the shop. Mother will be going with you and it'll be much safer in the countryside.' Hans who didn't really like school asked with a little smile on his face.

'What about school?' Hans knew we wouldn't be going back to school but he asked just to make sure.

'School will be closed till we get back because all your friends and all the children in the city will be going away too.' I looked at Mother and asked.

'How will we get to the countryside?'

'Everyone will be going on the train sometime soon but I'm not sure when and you boys should look forward to it. It's going to be a great adventure. Also before we leave we have to go to Berlin first to collect Grandmother and bring her back here with us, Grandmother will be coming with us to the countryside too.'

I thought to myself that it would be great to have her with us at the countryside because Grandmother was really funny. Grandmother always said really silly things and forgot everything she said so usually she would ask you the same question twice. Grandmother had an old wireless in her house and she thought that the man on the wireless was talking to her and asking her questions, so she would often spend the day talking to him and answering to everything he would say. I just think that maybe she was really lonely and had no one else to talk to.

I sat back and thought to myself. I'd never been to the countryside and I wasn't really in the mood for an adventure. I'd rather stay here in this house and stay here with my friends. I'd rather go to school and listen to the teacher ramble on, and listen to Siegfried Schulte asking silly questions about things he had no interest in and answering questions with silly answers just to make everyone laugh.

But it probably wasn't going to be safe because of all those planes flying over at night and all those bright flashes and loud rumbling noises I could hear from what sounded like just a few miles away. I know Father was telling us that they had just finished building the Bunkerkirche which was going to be a safe place for people to go at night when the planes were flying over. At least Father will be safe there at night when we're away at the countryside.

I thought what if we all ended up going on different trains to different parts of the countryside. How big was the countryside? Was it as big as our town and the city around it? Would everybody we know be on our train? Would Abigail Blaustein be on our train and go to the same countryside as us? At least that would be something good. Maybe I could ask her. But if I was to ask her, I'd have to do it before next week. Maybe I could try to ask her today. I just really hate the way everything keeps changing. Edward and Gustav had to leave for the war and I really miss them. Now we have to leave and Fathers not coming and I'm going to really miss him too. School is closed and I'm not going to see my friends for a while and I'm going to miss them too. Abigail Blaustein, I'll miss her even though I've never even spoken to her which is kind of strange if you think about it, but still I know I'll miss her.

We sat and ate breakfast that morning around our kitchen table without anybody saying anything. Everybody was just looking out the kitchen window at the snow falling and probably thinking about everything that was happening and worrying about where we were going and what was going to happen next. I was thinking about how long was this War going to last for, and when was our country going to be great again, because it didn't seem to be getting any better, only worse.

Chapter Four

My first Kiss

After breakfast Mother left for the shops and brought Hans with her, and Father, he left but didn't say where he was going just that I was in charge and I was to look after the shop. Now it wasn't very hard to look after the shop because nobody really came in anymore. The shop wasn't very big but I just loved everything about it. It had a large front window looking out onto the street which always seemed to be dusty no matter how much Father cleaned it. There was a brass bell hanging over the front door and every time the door opened it hit off the bell which made a really loud ringing sound that could be heard all over the house. We always knew when somebody was coming in to the shop. When the bell rang once you knew someone had come in and later when it rang a second time you were always curious as to whether that person had left or a second person had come in. It always got the better of me and no matter where I was in the house I had to go take a peek into the shop to see who was there.

All the book shelves in the shop were made from a dark coloured, hard grainy timber which was the same colour timber as in the window and the front door. There were shelves on every wall covered from top to bottom with hundreds of books about everything you could ever imagine. Most of the books I couldn't even reach they were so high up and you had to climb a ladder to get to them. Only the grownups were allowed climb the ladder to reach those books which were probably filled with words that children could never understand. One long book shelf sat in the middle of the floor which was about the same height as me, with books stacked tightly on both sides.

The floor was also made from wide dark timber floor boards. Boards that were so wide my foot could fit on the width of one board without touching the gaps on either side. We always called the gaps between the floor boards the cracks. Hans and I played a game where you never walked on the cracks but always kept your feet on the floor boards. Well it wasn't really a game but we just for some reason decided one day that you couldn't ever walk on the cracks. We did the same while walking outside on the footpaths. If you stepped on a crack you lost and the other person was the winner. So it became a habit never to walk on the cracks even when Hans wasn't there to shout. 'You walked on the cracks I win you lose.'

Near the front door and at the end of the book shelf in the middle of the floor, was a large red velvet chair for people to sit in to relax and read and decide if they were going to buy the book or not. Now this was my second favourite thing in the shop because it was just so soft and comfortable and it faced the front window which had the same great view that my bedroom window had. Only lower down of course and the people outside were much closer. Sometimes people would stand outside the front window looking in at the books in the window display, but mostly you would notice they were actually looking at their own reflection in the window. This was always very funny because they didn't know we were looking back at them. My absolute favourite thing about the shop was a secret kept from anybody who came in. Nobody knew about this only our family and maybe a few others but I'm not really sure who. Or maybe nobody knew. I can't be sure.

You see the end wall of the shop was actually just a line of book shelves right up to the ceiling that looked like it had nothing behind it when actually there was a room back there and there was a secret door built into the shelves. A small section of the shelves opened inwards and lead into that room which Father used as his office. The books on this section of shelves were always packed very tightly so as not to fall off when opening the door. Father was the only one who was allowed to open the door or enter his office. It was the only part of the house that was off limits which meant you couldn't go in no matter what. Sometimes when we played hide and seek we used to hide in the office but now it was off limits 'full stop.'

Mother used to say full stop sometimes at the end of a sentence like that when maybe she was telling us about a new rule. So Father was the only one who used the secret door but that was fine because it wouldn't be much of a secret I suppose if people just went in and out all of the time.

When Father had left this morning he asked me to clean dust from the books and shelves. I was in the middle of doing this with my back to the front door when I heard the bell ring. I turned to see who had just come in but I couldn't see anyone because the book shelf in the middle of the floor although around the same height as me was still blocking my view. I walked to the other side of the shelves towards the front window and looked down the length of the shop to see who was there. My heart nearly stopped, my body went numb. I got what can only be described as 'The shock of my life.' Standing there just inside the front door and looking straight at me with a small little smile on her face was Abigail Blaustein.

Abigail was wearing a white dress today that I have never seen her wear before and a white ribbon in her hair and both were the colour of snow. She wore her dark coloured coat which she never seemed to button up. The coat with the patch on the front in the shape of a yellow star and boots the same dark colour as her coat which were ankle height and were perfect for playing outside in this snowy weather. She had no gloves or hat, her long dark hair was tied back into a ponytail with shorts bits of hair still hanging on her forehead like a tiny fringe. Her face was pale almost white and her hands were red from the cold. She had dark coloured eyes maybe brown but I wasn't close enough to see properly, and bright red lips which were the colour of her dress that she normally wore. I thought she was beautiful and I wished I could tell her how I felt but I couldn't and I was never going to tell anybody how I felt about her.

Then the staring incident this morning came rushing into my head along with a hundred other things. My brain was racing like a race horse with all these thoughts coming in and going out. But I just couldn't think of what to say or what I had planned to say. I knew I had two questions I could ask her but they were gone. Then she said. 'Hello.'

I said nothing. She smiled and said. 'Isn't your name Deiter?' 'Yes and you're Abigail.' I spoke I couldn't believe it and I didn't stammer at all. I was so nervous and in such shock that I think my brain forgot to tell my mouth to stammer.

'Are you looking for a book?'
'Not really.' Abigail replied.
'I just came in to say hello.' Then I just remembered one of the questions. I was going to ask her about the yellow star on her coat but now for some reason and I don't know why, I didn't think it was the right thing to do. Then I remembered what Mother had been telling us this morning about all the women and children leaving the city.

'Are you going to the countryside next week?' I asked her.
'What do you mean the countryside?' She replied.
'Next week all the children in the city are going to the countryside on trains.' Abigail looked a little confused and said.

'Yes my Mother said we could be leaving soon but she never said we were going to the countryside, she never said where we were going.' I was just delighted to able to tell Abigail what was happening.

'Well it's the countryside that we're all going to, and we're not really happy about going, but we hope it's going to be a great adventure and we should be back in around six months.'

'Maybe Mother forgot to mention the countryside but she did say Father and I should have our bags packed because we would be going soon.'

Now I thought it was a little strange that our Father was staying behind and Abigail's Father was going to the countryside. But I wasn't going to mention it. It was confusing enough without bringing more questions into it. So I just asked Abigail the most important question.

'Do you think we might be going on the same train?' I was hoping she might try to convince her Mother to come on the same train as us.

'Maybe, I'll ask'. She replied. Abigail then walked closer and said. 'Have you ever been on a train?'

'No, I don't think so. Well I can't really remember ever being on a train or even being in a car in my life.'

'Would you like to take a walk to the train station tomorrow to see what the trains and the train station looks like?' Abigail asked. Now I couldn't believe it, Abigail Blaustein was asking me to go somewhere with her. So I said. 'Yes that sounds like a great Idea.' I was just so happy. This was the best day I'd had in a long time. I was talking to Abigail Blaustein and I wasn't stammering. And she never even mentioned the fact that I'd been staring out the window at her just that morning.

Then I thought to myself. I could show her the secret door in the book shelves. Surely she would be impressed. Abigail was standing now only about a step away and looking straight into my face and I into hers. I could now see that her eyes were a dark coloured brown, maybe the same colour as the book shelves and the front door but not quite as dark. My eyes were blue and most people I knew had blue eyes and I hadn't seen many brown eyes before but they were just beautiful probably the most beautiful eyes I'd ever seen.

Abigail was standing so close to me that I was starting to get nervous and I was afraid to talk just in case the stammer came back. I was getting the feeling now that there was an awkward silence and I better say something because the longer it lasted the worse it got. I took a deep breath and turned my back on her and walked towards the secret door. Now that we weren't face to face anymore, I was fine so I took a deep breath and I said as fast as I could.

'Would you like to see the secret door?'

'Secret door, what do you mean secret door?' Abigail replied. I turned again and faced her. I was standing in front of the secret door with my hands on the book shelf and I said.

'We have a secret door and it's hidden in the shelves.'

I pushed the book shelves inwards and the secret door opened. Abigail looked surprised and then walked straight past me into the office behind the secret door. I stepped inside the office too and looked around. I hadn't been in here for a long time because Mother and Father had said it was off limits. We both stood there looking around us. The office was small with a table and two chairs. It had lots of books that needed fixing on shelves much the same as the ones in the shop but just not as nice. Abigail looked at me and with a smile on her face she said. 'This is really nice. I wish we had a room like this in our house behind a secret door. What a brilliant hiding place.' We sat on the two chairs in Father's office which were facing each other and with Father's large office table between us.

'Did you see the fire in the town square last night?' I asked.

'No. What do you mean a fire, was there a house on fire?'

'No. There was a fire in the middle of the square near the statue of the horse with a man on his back. And it was very strange because they were burning books. Nothing only books. Everybody there was throwing books on the fire, even the soldiers.' Abigail looked at me with a confused look on her face. The same look that Hans had on his face and probably the same look that I had on my face while looking at the fire last night.

'Why were they burning books?' Abigail asked, now with a confused tone also.

'I'm not really sure but it was such a waste of books.' I didn't mention that I thought it was a waste of heat too because that would just sound silly.

'What do you think of the soldiers uniforms aren't they really smart?'

'Yes I suppose.' Abigail replied but not sounding very convincing. So I decided to tell her.

'They need lots of soldiers in smart uniforms to make our country great again.' I said it but I didn't really believe it because nothing seemed to be getting any better only worse. Then Abigail said sounding more convincing this time. 'I don't really like the soldiers. They always look at me as if they don't like me so I just hide or keep away from them when I see them.'

So I thought to myself, I better not mention that Edward and Gustav were soldiers and wore those really smart uniforms. But I did want to tell Abigail that they were gone away and we didn't really know where they were anymore and that I really missed them. But I couldn't tell her now because I knew she didn't like soldiers and maybe Abigail might think that I was going to become a soldier and be really mean too. So I thought to myself that I shouldn't say anything and just talk about something different.

'I always get dressed under the blankets in the morning because it's so cold.'

'Yes.' Abigail replied and said no more. I said that thinking it was so clever but it actually ended up sounding silly and then I thought it would probably remind her of the staring out the bedroom window incident this morning. Damn it, now she was probably thinking the same thing and I brought it up. Now once again I had to think of something else to talk about to get her mind off that very embarrassing incident.

Abigail wasn't talking very much. Maybe she was shy and maybe she was just as shy as I was or maybe just as nervous as I was about saying something silly. I never mentioned the yellow star on her coat. I don't know why but I just got a bad feeling about it and a feeling that she didn't like it. When I looked at the star, Abigail always tried to cover it with her hand. It really was the strangest thing that so many were wearing this patch on their clothes for no reason. No reason that I could think of anyway. Then Abigail spoke which was music to my ears.

'Do you know how to get to the train station?'

I thought to myself for just a second about where the train station was or had I ever passed by it at any stage while out walking with Mother or Father. Or maybe on one of our adventures that Hans and I used to take around the town or sometimes the city beyond that.

'I don't think I've ever seen the train station but I'm sure we will be able to find it if we ask somebody how to get there. I hope it's not on the other side of the river because the river is just so wide and the bridge so long and it's always so windy and freezing cold when you walk across the bridge.'

'Will you still come with me if it's across the bridge?' Abigail asked with a little anxious look on her face.

'Of course I will. Don't worry we'll find it, it can't be that far away.' There was no way I was going to miss an adventure with Abigail Blaustein. I was looking forward to it already and I didn't care if we had to cross ten bridges, I was going. I would run away with Abigail Blaustein right now if I could, and get a little house together and as it always said at the end of the books we read in school or the books in Fathers shop. We would

'Live happily ever after'

Then Abigail looked at me in a strange way because I think she could see I was daydreaming and she asked. 'What time do you think we should leave at?' 'I think we could leave at eight o clock in the morning if we wanted. Just to make sure we get there and back again. Mother always wakes us before eight anyway.'

'That sounds perfect. I will call over to the shop in the morning.'

I then had this image in my head of Abigail Blaustein standing in our book shop and Mother asking her questions about where we were going. Father saying you're not going to any train station. And Hans standing behind them laughing and probably blowing kisses at us, as some sort of a joke, which was like something he would do. So I said.

'I think we should meet outside on the street so nobody asks us any questions about where we are going.'

'Yes that sounds better because Mother might not be happy with me if she hears I'm going to another part of the city.' Abigail replied.

Just then we heard footsteps and noises at the front door. I jumped up and closed the secret door. We heard the sound of the shop door opening and the bell that hangs over it gave a loud ringing sound. The shop door closed and the bell rang again. We could hear voices in the shop so we knew that two people had come in. We peeked through the gaps in the book shelves and we could see clearly out into the shop. It was Mother and Hans that had just come in and they were standing at the front door wiping their feet on the door mat and taking off their coats while having a little chat. They were probably wondering where I was gone and if they weren't well they soon would be. They both headed across the shop floor towards the kitchen at the back of the house. I watched closely to see if Hans would step on the cracks of the timber floors, but much to my amazement he never stepped on one. Hans has like myself developed the same habit to never walk on the cracks. I was glad he didn't walk on the cracks because I couldn't just jump out from behind the book shelves and shout. 'You walked on the cracks, I win you lose.' Now that would look just a little weird and with Abigail Blaustein standing beside me.

Mother and Hans went out the door of the shop and across the hall and past the stairs and into the kitchen. Abigail turned to me and said.

'I have to go now. I have to go home. I will see you tomorrow at eight outside the shop.'

'Yes.' I said. 'I'll see you tomorrow outside. I'm really looking forward to it'.

I opened the secret door for us to leave and then Abigail turned to me and without warning gave me a kiss on the cheek at the edge of my lips and left the office, walked across the shop floor, walking on all the cracks and went out the front door which left the bell over the door ringing loudly.

I was stuck to the floor. I was shocked, shaking a little and smiling a little too. She kissed me. Why did she kiss me? Why does it matter, she kissed me that was the important thing. Well this had just turned out to be the best day of my life. I had a strange feeling in my chest and stomach. Not a pain but just a strange good feeling. Abigail Blaustein had kissed me, my first kiss. I couldn't believe it. This day had started out so bad, Abigail seeing me staring at her through the window, which was so embarrassing but which she had never mentioned. We were told we had to leave home to go to the countryside and without Father.

But now everything was perfect and everything looked so much better now. All the things I had to worry about and there was a lot. Well I couldn't even remember any of them anymore and I still had tomorrow to look forward to. I feel as if I could do anything and I think I could be in love but I'm not sure because I've never been in love before. And they don't teach you in school how it feels to be in love.

I closed the office door and went across the shop floor and into the hall way and passed the stairs and into the kitchen to where Mother and Hans were. Now I can't even remember if I'd walked on the cracks on the shop floor or not.

Like Abigail, it was as if I was oblivious to the game of not walking on the cracks. But it didn't matter to me anymore about cracks on floors or cracks on footpaths, dust on bookshelves, yellow stars, red flags or going to the countryside for I had just been kissed by Abigail Blaustein.

Chapter five
January 28th 1942
Day Three
The soldiers and The Animal Trains.

I was awake the next morning, long before Mother had to call me. I got dressed under the blankets as usual because once again it was freezing outside and close to freezing in my bedroom. I jumped out of bed and went straight to the small dormer window which was, like yesterday morning frozen on the inside. And like yesterday morning with the side of my fist I started rubbing in circles as hard and as fast as I could. I kept going until I had made a clear circle in the glass to look out through. Just like yesterday, Abigail was outside on the street playing but only this morning she was alone. It was too early yet for any of her friends to have called. I was looking down at Abigail playing on the street and then once again like yesterday and without warning she looked back at me. My heart skipped a beat, but this morning I didn't mind that she could see me looking at her. I waved and she smiled and waved back at me. I held up my pointing finger to her as a signal to say I'd be out in one minute. I think she understood because she smiled at me once again and nodded her head at me as if to say yes. I ran down the stairs as quick as I could and into the kitchen where

Mother was sitting at the kitchen table having breakfast. Mother gave me some breakfast and we sat together eating.

Father was still in bed but he would be up shortly to open the shop as usual. He'd always open the shop by unlocking the door, but then he'd always go back and have his breakfast in the kitchen. Knowing that when he heard the bell over the door ring, somebody had just come in and then he could go help them pick out a good book to read.

'Why are you up so early'? Mother asked.

'No reason. I couldn't really sleep.' I replied.

'Are you worried about having to go to the countryside?'

'Not really. I'm sort of looking forward to it. It might be a great adventure, travelling on a train and all.'

Now I thought this could be a perfect opportunity to find out where exactly the train station was. I didn't fancy stopping strangers on the street, and asking them how to get to the train station. Some people for some reason would answer a question with a question. If you asked them how to get somewhere, they would reply by asking. 'Why is a little boy like you going there?' Which was pretty annoying because that always led to another list of questions that ended up with them knowing who I was, knowing I lived on Bilker Street, what my Father's name was and what my Mother's name was. And finally a story about how they went to school with my parents or maybe even my grandparents. And then you'd end up just smiling and you'd be no further on, on your adventure or in finding the place that you were going.

'Have you ever been on a train?' I asked.

'Of course I have. I've been on trains many times and they're really nice and I know you're going to enjoy it.' I paused and thought and waited and then I asked.

'Where is the train station? Is it far away?'

'Not far at all. It should only take us about twenty minutes to walk there.' Now that didn't work. I still didn't know where the train station was. Now I'll have to ask another question while trying not to sound too obsessed about it. I waited for a few seconds and thought of what to say.

'Is it on the other side of the river? I don't like crossing over the long bridge, it's always really cold on the bridge.' Mother looked at me happily and said.

'You'll be fine Deiter. It's in the opposite direction.' So now I had an idea as to where we were going and it was only going to take twenty minutes to get there. We should be able to get there and back without anybody even knowing we are gone. Although I didn't mind if it took all day because I'd be with Abigail and that was just the perfect way to spend a day. I finished my breakfast and jumped up while saying. 'I'm going outside for a while.' I grabbed my coat which was hanging on the post at the bottom of the stairs, ran through the shop, avoiding the cracks in the floor, unlocked the front door and ran outside. Forgetting how loud the bell over the door was and knowing that I had probably woken everyone in the house. Abigail was waiting outside on the street for me. She was wearing her white dress and a white ribbon in her hair and her dark coloured coat with the yellow star on it and her brown boots. She smiled and said. 'Hello.'

I smiled back and said. 'Hello.'

I wasn't sure if we were supposed kiss when we met or was last night's kiss just a once off. Or a dream or something I had imagined. Or were we only supposed to kiss when she was leaving or were we ever going to kiss again. I wasn't sure if we were boyfriend and girlfriend or just friends or what was happening. I decided to say nothing about it because at the moment I was just happy to be with her.

We headed off together down the street towards the town square, the one with the town hall covered in those red flags with the white circle and the strange black sign in the middle, red flags that were bigger than any other flags in our town. The town square with the clock tower and the statue of the horse with the man on his back. All the streets in town were made from cobble stones, the narrow streets, and the wide streets which also had tram lines. Now this time of year we couldn't see the cobbles or the tram lines because the snow was just too deep. The buildings on the narrow streets were mostly two storeys high like on our street and the buildings on the wider streets were three storeys high and sometimes four. The streets were extra quiet this morning because it was so early and most people were probably still in bed.

We arrived at the town square which was also pretty quiet with only a few people standing around talking and some walking briskly as if in a hurry to get somewhere important. Now we weren't sure as to which street we should take next out of the square to get to the station. We had three choices, three streets that left the square in three different directions. Four if you counted the one we were standing on, but we knew it wasn't back that way. I looked at Abigail and she looked back at me, both of us looking a little confused but not looking overly worried in any way for our adventure had only begun. 'Which street do you think we have to take next?' Abigail asked me.

'I don't really know but I think it's one of those two over there, because they both go in the opposite direction to the river, and Mother said the road to the train station went that way.'
'Do you think we should ask somebody?' Abigail asked.
'I think so, let's go, we'll ask one of those old people in the middle of the square.' We started walking down across the square together and I turned to Abigail and said. 'It's always best to ask somebody old because they have been around for such a long time that they know how to get everywhere. Old people are always much friendlier too because I think they're glad to have somebody to talk to and they always have the time to talk because they're never in a hurry to get anywhere.'

'That's true.' Abigail replied.
'I hope we don't have to ask any soldiers how to get there because I don't really like soldiers.' Once again I thought of Edward and Gustav who were away at the war and thought to myself, I better not ever mention them.

We slowed down near the middle of the square when we seen two old ladies standing talking. There always seemed to be old ladies standing talking and never old men, there just seemed to be a lot less old men in our town. We slowly walked towards them and asked as politely as possible.

47

'Could you tell us how we could get to the train station please?' Abigail stood behind me as if she were hiding, she looked a little frightened but I'm not sure why. One of them replied. 'The Station, why are you going to the station?' I asked a question and as usual they answered with a question. Maybe they just want to have a conversation and they don't really care why or where we're going. 'We're meeting my Grandmother who's coming from Berlin on the train'. Now that was a lie of course but it doesn't really matter, because we just have to tell them something. Old people just like to hear some sort of news even if it's not true, because if like my Grandmother they'll probably have it forgotten in five minutes. I could feel Abigail smiling behind me now and I thought at least she's not frightened anymore.

'The station is straight down that street there about fifteen or twenty minutes away.' One of the old ladies said pointing at the street at the bottom end of the square going in the opposite direction to the river just like Mother had said. 'Thank you very much.' I said and we started to walk towards our street. 'Say hello to your grandmother for me.' The old lady said with a big smile on her face as if she knew something that we didn't know. We walked across the rest of the square passed where the fire was on Monday evening, but the ground was now covered in snow and there was no sign of it anymore just like it had never happened. Sometimes things seem like they never happened or that you just dreamed them up in your head or it was a story you heard. I didn't mention it to Abigail now because all proof of it had vanished. We walked towards the street at the bottom end of the square. The street in the middle of the square was a narrow street, but the one we were going down now was a much wider street. We walked along for about five minutes just talking about different things we could see around us. The cobble stones, the flags, the tall buildings, the people, the shops, the shop window displays, the trams, the fact that everything just seemed to be grey and white. The trams were parked in different areas all along the street but none of them were moving or being used. There were a few more people walking up and down this street than there was in the town square.

'What do you think of all the flags?' I asked Abigail.

'They're just a bit unusual. I like the colour but the thing in the middle just looks silly I think.'

'Yes that's true alright, I don't know what it means or why they have them everywhere and every time I ask, nobody will tell me.'

'Maybe nobody knows.' Abigail replied. 'Maybe you're right.'

We walked down that long street towards the station talking and I, happier than I have ever been. I didn't care how long it took us to get there, or how cold it was, or how long this street was because walking along talking to Abigail Blaustein was all my dreams come true. She always smiled at everything I said, and she knew something about everything we talked about. The only time Abigail seemed unhappy was when we passed a soldier on the street. Abigail sort of hid behind me when we passed them. When we finally got to the bottom of that street we had two choices, left or right. The old lady in the town square hadn't mentioned anything about us having to turn right or left to get to the station. People now were moving up and down much faster as if they were on a mission or had somewhere important to go. All moving much faster than anyone was in the town square. There wasn't a single old person to be seen anywhere to ask how we'd get to the station from here. Hopefully we haven't gone in the wrong direction all together. Hopefully the old lady in the square has given us the right directions. We stood on the corner of the street just looking around us wondering where to go next. Just then Abigail jumped, shouted and pointed all at once. 'Look! The sign it's pointing that way.' I looked up and yes there it was a sign that read. 'Dusseldorf Derendorf Freight Station.' It was such a relief knowing we hadn't gone in completely the wrong direction. We started off on our journey once again down a much narrower street now but still much the same as all the other streets. I thought to myself Freight Station, Train Station, what was the difference? And then away in the distance we could see what looked like an entrance to a train station or an entrance to something big.

The street was much busier now than any of the other streets we were on. There were people walking now in both directions on the footpaths. It was a little harder now to see where you were going and everybody we met just kept saying. 'Excuse me. Excuse me.' There were a lot more soldiers around now too. Abigail grabbed my hand and held it tightly as we walked with our heads down as if in a hurry, just like everybody else. At the end of the street we finally came to the train station. This large building was straight in front of us now and facing back up the street we had just come down. We knew it had to be the train station because either side of the main building and in the

distance we could see what looked like trains. And on the main building up high over our heads was a sign that read.
'Dusseldorf Derendorf Freight Station.'
Now that we had reached the train station, we were still a little confused because the sign over the station read Freight Station.

'Maybe Freight Station means the same thing as Train Station.' I said to Abigail. 'I've never heard of a Freight Station, but surely it has to be the same thing. This is the way the old lady in the Town Square told us to go.' Abigail replied.

Outside the station there was a line of soldiers standing to attention. Every soldier had a large dog on a lead. A large very mean looking brown and black dog with pointed ears, dogs that never seemed to sit but rather just keep walking across and back in front of the soldier, and from time to time jumping up and barking at really nothing in particular.

We decided not to go in the main entrance of the station because we would have to pass the soldiers and their very mean looking dogs. I knew Abigail didn't like soldiers and I didn't really like these soldiers either or their dogs. They didn't look like my two brothers Edward and Gustav that had gone away to the War. These soldiers looked like they could never smile and Edward and Gustav were always smiling. We crossed over to the other side of the street and went down a little passed the Station, where we could see a wire fence that we might be able look through.

When we both got there we stood with our hands holding onto the fence, our hands up high beside our faces and our faces pressed against the wire looking through at the Station and all the trains. We couldn't see one train that looked like it was for carrying small children to the countryside. All the trains in there were animal trains. There were four or maybe five tracks in the station and even the trains in the distance were animal trains. All the trains were really old looking, made from what looked like old planks of wood and painted in black, green or red with the paint now peeling off them. The wheels were brown and rusty looking like they could fall apart at any minute, and they looked as if they couldn't move anymore, but would have been very useful for carrying animals maybe fifty years ago.

The snow was now falling gently and it was bitterly cold. It was as cold here and as breezy as it would be when you were on the bridge crossing over the wide river. The snow was about the size of my foot deep and looked even deeper piled on top of the trains. We could hear lots of muffled sounds coming from the station platform. We couldn't see in the direction of the platform but we knew there were lots of people in there.

'Why are there people in the train station? And no trains for the people to go on.' Abigail asked.

'Maybe the train has to come yet.' Now I hadn't even thought of that until Abigail asked, but now I knew.

'We should try to find a way into the station to get a closer look at the nice train when it arrives. I really would like to see what it looks like before we have to travel on it next week going to the countryside.' 'Yes me too.' Abigail replied.
'I will have to ask Mother if we can travel on the same day as you next week and hopefully on the same train too. We'll have

such a great time in the countryside when we get there and some great adventures too.'

'That sounds like a great idea. I just can't wait to get there and I would say it's always going to be warm in the countryside because the farmers have to grow things and the cows and sheep have to sleep outside.' Abigail replied. The countryside is going to be just like heaven I thought to myself.

We walked further down the street to where we could see a gap in the fence that both of us could fit through. I pulled the wire back on one side towards me and made the gap even bigger and told Abigail to climb through. Abigail climbed through carefully making sure not to catch her coat in the fence and I followed. We were now both inside the station and walked along the wire fence, back towards the main building only this time on the inside of the fence which made me a little nervous. We were closer now to the main building than where we were while looking through the fence just a few minutes ago.

We could see an old lookout tower now around fifteen steps away, out in the direction of the train tracks and away from the fence, which were at the same level as we were walking. We were about four or maybe five of my feet below the platform which we still couldn't really see clearly yet. We walked slowly out towards the tower which looked as old as the trains and was also made of old timber planks of wood. The tower had a rusty old stairs leading up the side of it to a door which we couldn't be sure was locked or not. As we walked towards the tower we kept our eyes to the left watching out to make sure we weren't seen because we knew we would soon be coming into view of the people on the platform. We walked slowly and quietly, a little hunched down and the only sound that could be heard was the sound of crunching snow under our feet which wasn't loud enough to give us away but sounded loud enough to make us even more nervous than we already were.

Finally we got to the corner of the old tower on the opposite side to the platform. We were now safe and out of sight of the people. We were at the bottom of the old rusty stairs that led to the doorway of the tower. We moved quietly once again around the bottom of the stairs and back in tight to the side of the tower and under the stairs. We took a few more steps towards the front side of the tower which faced the railway tracks. When we got there we stopped and I turned to Abigail and whispered.

'If we go any further out past this tower we'll be seen from the platform for sure.' Abigail whispered.

'You'll have to take a quick look around the corner to see if any soldiers are on the platform. Do it as fast as you can and don't get caught.'

I very slowly stuck my head out around the corner and I could see hundreds of people waiting on the platform. I pulled my head back as fast as I could because there were so many people up there that I couldn't be sure if any of them were looking back at me. I turned to Abigail and whispered.

'There must be hundreds of people up there on the platform but I can't really see who they are, or if any of them are soldiers or children going to the countryside.'

We decided to go back now to the bottom of the stairs and make our way slowly to the top to see if the door of the tower was open. We walked slowly up the stairs being as careful as we could not to make a sound or slip and fall. At the top of the stairs we pushed hard on the door and it opened. We went inside and closed the door behind us. It felt much warmer in the tower because you could no longer feel the cold breeze blowing. The windows of the tower were just above our eye level so it was just perfect for peeking out. The windows were a little frozen on the outside, but not too bad on the inside unlike my bedroom window which always had ice on the inside. The tower had timber floors much the same as the book shop floor only wider and I made sure not to walk on the cracks. We were now up very high and had a perfect view of the platform and everybody on it. We still had to keep very quiet so we wouldn't be heard.

There must have been at least one thousand men and women of all ages, young and old, and at least one hundred children standing in the freezing cold on the platform surrounded by soldiers. Soldiers just like outside the station with large brown and black dogs that were jumping and barking and trying to get away. The dogs were barking and trying to get away towards the people waiting for the train to arrive. Abigail and I looked at each other both not knowing what was happening. This was as strange and even more confusing than the fire in the town square Monday evening. All of these people were standing crammed together on the platform, nobody talking or moving, and looking maybe even a little afraid. Most of the people were carrying small suit cases, which didn't look like they could hold very much. Not much good if you're travelling to the countryside for at least six months. This was one of the strangest things I'd ever seen. Nobody looked like they even wanted to be there or that they were in the least bit happy to be going on a train to the countryside. The soldiers looked very mean and they seemed to be acting like they didn't even like the people waiting for the train. How was it even any business of the soldiers or why were they standing there as if they were guarding the people? I turned to Abigail and whispered.

'Do you know what's happening?' Abigail was looking just as confused as I was. 'I don't know.' Abigail replied.

It was then that I noticed that everybody on the platform was wearing those patches of the yellow star on their clothes. Most had the yellow star on their coats at the front just like Abigail but some had the patch on their back nearly on their shoulder. Now I didn't know what to say to Abigail and I didn't know if she had noticed it. Just then a man started to run away in our direction, he was running as fast as he could but still he didn't seem to be getting very far and then he turned left and out across the railway tracks. Once again Abigail and I looked at each other surprised and then.

BANG!
We both jumped and looked back to see the man was now lying face down on the tracks. We hadn't seen him fall but we could see him now lying on the ground looking like he was just a pile of black clothes.

'What happened?' Abigail asked.

'I think he was shot.' Now Father had a gun in his office table drawer which used to belong to Grandfather, and which I had seen lots of times, but I'd only ever heard it being fired once before and that is exactly what it sounded like.

'Who shot him?' Abigail asked.
'One of the soldiers I think.'
I was starting now to feel a little bit sick because I was so frightened and feeling like we were no longer safe in this tower. I knew we shouldn't be in here or we shouldn't have seen what we just seen or what had just happened right in front of our eyes. I was in shock now and didn't know what we were going to do. I hardly had the strength to go back down the steps of the tower. I stood completely still looking out through the window. None of the people on the platform moved or tried to go out to help the man on the tracks. I could now hear people crying and then two of the soldiers slowly walked out to the body and dragged him back to where he had come from and left him on the ground at the end of the platform. The soldiers were struggling to keep the dogs from getting away. I still hadn't mentioned to Abigail that everyone on the platform had yellow stars just like hers and I didn't really know if I should mention it or if Abigail had noticed it herself.

I thought to myself as I stood there in the tower looking out, that this was the most horrible thing I'd ever seen. The snow was getting much heavier now, so much heavier that I could barely see out and I could barely see the station and the platform anymore.

I whispered to Abigail.
'I think we should leave now while the snow is heavy and they

probably can't see us.' I was more worried now about been seen than I was earlier. Earlier it was an adventure but now it felt like a nightmare. I looked back towards the station and my heart jumped and I felt sick. One of the soldiers was coming towards us with his dog on a lead. The dog was barking up in the direction of the tower as if he knew we were in here and he probably did know because dogs can hear everything even things we can't hear. Abigail sat down on the floor of the tower and put her head between her knees and her hands over her ears. She had seen the soldier too coming towards us and had gotten such a fright she probably couldn't stand. I sat down now too beside Abigail and I could hear the soldier and his dog getting closer. I thought to myself that dogs have a great sense of smell and he could probably have picked up our scent by now. I could hear them at the bottom of the stairs, the dog barking now so loudly that you couldn't hear that Abigail had started crying. Surely the soldier could see our footsteps in the snow coming from the fence towards the tower and up the steps to the door. I didn't know what we were going to say if the soldier came up to us. Abigail looked up at me with tears coming down her now very pale face and whispered.

'I have a star on my coat just like all the people on the platform.'

 I didn't know what to say. I didn't want to say anything. I wanted to tell her everything would be fine but I couldn't make a sound and I wasn't sure if everything was going to be fine.

The soldier was now walking up the steps of the tower very slowly. It sounded like he hadn't got the dog with him. It sounded as if he'd tied the dog at the bottom of the stairs. I sat closer to Abigail now and I put my arm around her shoulder and my head against hers. She was shaking even more than I was. I looked up and could see the shadow of the soldier at the door but he wasn't trying to open the door. He was trying to look through the glass in the door which was frozen over. He had his hands by the side of his face like two wings and his face pressed against the glass. He then started to rub the glass with the side of his fist just like I have to do in the morning on my dormer window. He spent at least a minute rubbing the glass and he had a perfect circle defrosted at eye level to look through. The dog was still barking at the bottom of the steps and it sounded as if he was trying to come up the stairs to find us because he knew for sure that we were in here. The soldier turned and shouted back down at him to be quiet. He turned towards the glass again and put his two hands back up to the sides of his face like two wings and pressed his nose and hands against the glass. He was looking through the glass for a couple of seconds and probably trying to focus his eyes on the inside of the tower. He looked around the room and I'm not sure how, but he didn't see us and then I could hear shouting now coming from what sounded like the direction of the platform. The soldier went back down the stairs and we could hear his feet crunching in the snow and getting further away from us with the dog still barking as loud as ever.

We could hear a train coming in the distance which was drowning out the sound of the dog barking and which was music to my ears. We slowly stood up again very quietly and still shaking with fear. We peeked out the window again to see that the snow wasn't as bad as before and that the soldier and his dog was just arriving back at the platform.

The train was getting closer and the dogs on the platform were getting more excited. The train came from the far side of the station pulled in with the sound of screeching brakes and steam rising up in the air. It was coming in our direction and it kept moving and didn't stop until it had completely passed the platform and stopped just out in front of the lookout tower just below us. Now while this was happening an old lady had started walking away from the platform and was walking in our direction. Nobody had even noticed as everyone was busy looking at the train. Not even the dogs noticed her walking away. She walked past the tower and over to fence now out of sight of the platform. She followed the fence along in the same direction as we had just come in. She climbed out through the gap in the fence that we came through and walked away down the street until we couldn't see her anymore through the falling snow. I was amazed at what had just happened but hadn't time to think any more about it.

We looked down now at the train and just like all the other trains, this was an animal train that just pulled into the station. It looked just as old with planks of wood for the walls and rusty old wheels that looked as if they weren't going to be moving very fast. The soldiers came down from the platform and went along the train opening the large doors on the sides of the train. When all the doors had been opened the soldiers started ordering the people down off the platform and they made them walk along beside the train towards the front. When the people got to the door nearest the front of the train they were told to get in. Now, all the way from the front of the train to the back, the crowds of people were climbing into the train which wasn't very easy because there weren't any steps to use. Men were climbing in, turning around and taking suit cases from the people on the ground and then helping to pull them up. Everyone was helping lift the children up and trying to help the older men and women too. It looked as if there wasn't going to be enough room on this train for everybody so some were going to have to stay behind and wait for another one which meant we might have to hide in here for even longer.

Old men were arguing with the soldiers and one old lady was on her knees on the ground. It looked like she couldn't stand up anymore. One of the soldiers came over and kept shouting at her until after about thirty seconds he stood behind her, took out his gun and pointed it at the back of her head. He was shouting but I couldn't hear exactly what he was saying. Abigail covered her face with her hands and started to cry. The soldier pulled the trigger. A loud bang and the lady fell forward. Abigail started to cry now even harder and sat back down on the floor once again. Another man came running over and the soldier turned and pointed his gun at him too, he shouted at him as if ordering him to stop and when the man got closer the soldier again pulled the trigger and once again a loud bang and the man fell to the ground. The soldiers were now hitting people and pointing guns at anyone that looked like they were going to step out of line even though there were no lines or any sort of order to what was happening. The trains looked like they should be full now at this stage but they kept forcing more and more people into the carriages. More guns were used and more people lay on the ground. The soldiers were hitting people so hard that some were falling and some weren't getting back up again. The dogs were attacking people as they tried to climb on board and the soldiers just let them. It now looked like this was going to be the only train and everyone was going to be made travel on this one.

I sat down now on the floor beside Abigail. I didn't know what to say to her. She had her hands in her face and was crying. I just put my arm around her and stayed silent. This couldn't be explained or talked about. We sat there listening to what was still happening outside. We could hear the people screaming and crying. We could hear the soldiers shouting and the dogs barking. We could still hear the gunshots and a scream each time afterwards. I was still feeling sick and couldn't wait to get out of here and go home to the shop and sit in the red chair and read a book and look out the window at the people passing up and down the street. I looked up at the sky through the window and just watched the snow falling and listened and hoped it would end soon. But it just seemed to last forever. After a while I could hear the train starting to move. I stood up and once again peeked out through the window. The train was starting to move out of the station. Everybody had been crammed onto the one train.

Nobody left behind only the dead bodies on the ground. I could see there were gaps near the roof of the train and I could see faces looking out through as if trying to grab a breath of fresh air.
After the sound of the train had faded into the distance the soldiers stood talking and smoking cigarettes right beside the lookout tower. We once again sat down as quietly as possible and listened to the soldiers outside laughing and talking like nothing had ever happened. The smell of the cigarette smoke which I usually didn't mind and reminded me of Grandfather was now making me feel sick again.

The dogs were barking as loud as ever but the soldiers just ignored them. Before the soldiers left we heard them say that another train was due to pull into the station that afternoon, and they had to have everyone there ready to go by then no excuses. Unless the train is full it's a waste I heard one of the soldiers say.

The soldiers left and went back to the platform and then back to the street in front of the station. Abigail and I climbed back down from the tower, down the old steps and back to the fence where we had come in. We climbed through the fence onto the street once again and walked by the station where the soldiers were standing and back up the very busy narrow street with our heads down trying not to be noticed. We now knew that we had something to fear, that morning we had everything to look forward to but now we knew things were different. All these soldiers in their smart uniforms were needed to make this country great again but now I didn't know what to think or what was happening or how putting people on animal trains was going to make things better or killing people for no reason at all was going to make our country great again. I didn't know how I was going to explain this to Mother and Father. Would they even believe me?

When we turned back onto the street that brought us straight back up to the old town square where the old lady had given us directions to which I am guessing was the wrong station, I noticed Abigail was no longer wearing her coat. I hadn't noticed what she had done with it. We hadn't spoken now since we were back in the tower so I decided not to say anything yet. Sometimes it is best not to say anything when you know somebody doesn't want to talk and I knew I could ask Abigail

later. At the moment we were both still in shock and I knew Abigail getting rid of her coat had something to do with the yellow star. I took off my coat and gave it to Abigail and she put it on and just said thank you.
We just couldn't wait to get home now.

Then as we walked, in the distance we could see hundreds of people coming slowly down the middle of the wide street in our direction. We stopped and now once again we were looking at each other in shock. We stood back into a shop front door way. We stood and watched as hundreds of people passed by very slowly each one carrying a small suit case or some maybe two suit cases. They were surrounded and being told what to do by the soldiers. We knew where they were going and what was happening. All of these people were heading towards the station to be put into the animal trains again and once again all of them had yellow stars on their coats. As it came to an end, at the back of the crowd there were around ten soldiers following them with those large brown and black dogs that were barking and jumping trying to get away. It was then that Abigail put her hand on my shoulder and pointed to the crowd and screamed.

'IT'S MOTHER AND FATHER'!

Chapter Six

Hiding Abigail

When I woke this morning I felt as if this was going to be the best day of my life. I knew I was going on an adventure with Abigail Blaustein. I knew that I was looking forward so much to going to the countryside. I knew that Abigail had kissed me on the cheek the day before. I knew things were changing and I knew that everything was only getting better. But now as I stood in this shop front door on this freezing cold January day looking at the soldiers shouting and the dogs barking. Abigail's Mother and Father marching with the hundreds of other people towards the freight station to be put onto the animal trains. I knew that this wasn't to be the best day of my life but rather the worst I had ever seen.

Abigail didn't know what to do and neither did I. If she ran into the street to her Mother and Father she knew she would be forced to go to the animal trains. If she didn't she knew she might never see them again. Abigail turned to me and said. 'I better go with them or....' I grabbed Abigail by the arm and said. 'Let's go before you end up having to go on the animal train too.' We left there as fast as we could. We went back through the old town square and back to the book shop.

I ran inside while Abigail went to her house to see what was happening. I ran so fast that the bell over the front door fell down and hit the floor with a loud ringing sound that stopped a lot faster than it would if it were still hanging over the door.

'Mother, Father you won't believe what I've seen today.'

Mother and Father were both standing in the shop looking at books and Han's was sitting back in the red chair just relaxing but not reading a book. When I looked at how happy and peaceful everyone was, I now wished I had never gone anywhere this morning.

'Mother, Father we went for a walk to the train station today to see if.'

'Wait just one minute now Deiter. Who went to the station and who went with you?' Mother asked.

'Abigail.' I said looking and waiting for a reaction from everyone. The only reaction I got was from Han's who was blowing kisses and thinking he was really funny. Father smiled when he seen him.

'We went to the station to see what the trains looked like. The trains we would be going on to the countryside.' I said as fast as I could in hope that no more questions would be asked about Abigail, but rather about the train station.

'And what did you see?' Mother asked.

'When we got there all they had were nothing only animal trains, animal trains but no trains for people to go on. But then they made hundreds of people maybe even a thousand people get onto an animal train and they even shot some of the people if they didn't get on the train fast enough.' Now I wasn't sure exactly why they had shot some of the people but I had to tell Mother and Father about it and give some reason as to why I thought they had shot them.

Abigail was now standing outside on the street looking towards the shop waiting for me to come out. I ran outside to Abigail and told her to come in, and that I was explaining to Mother and Father what we had seen. Abigail said to me with tears streaming down her face and in a shaky voice.

'They're gone and all their clothes too. They have left without me.' We went back inside now where Father was picking up the bell from the floor and trying to put it all back together again. As we walked in Hans was being ordered to his bedroom which he didn't look very happy about, but I'm sure he'd be listening carefully from the top of the stairs which Hans and I always did.

'Abigail's Father and Mother are gone now too. We saw them being marched to the station by the soldiers and the dogs.' Mother sat down now on the red chair and looked at Abigail and I.

'Let's just slow things down now for one minute and answer me one question at a time. Who were the people getting on the train?'

'We don't know who they were, but every one of them had a patch of a yellow star on their coat and some were shot for no reason.' I said to mother as calmly as I could and now saying they were shot for no reason because they really were shot for no real reason. Mother looked at me a little bewildered and then over at Father. Father then asked. 'What station did you go to?' I looked at Abigail because I couldn't remember the exact name of the station.

'What was the name of the station Abigail?' Abigail shrugged her shoulders and said.

'I can't remember but the sign had freight station on it.'

'Yes Father that was it. Dusseldorf freight station.'

'And who shot the people at the train station?' Mother asked.

'The soldiers shot them. And on the way back we saw more people being brought to the station by the soldiers and the big brown and black dogs and Abigail's Father and Mother were with them.'

'Do you know where your Mother and Father are today Abigail?' Mother asked.

'They're gone to the station with the soldiers but I didn't know they were going and I am probably supposed to be with them. All I knew was that we were to go away soon but I'm not really sure where or when we were going.'

I looked at Abigail and she looked really pale and sick, she looked as though she was about to collapse at any second. Mother stood up and said. 'Abigail sit down here in this chair you look exhausted. I'll get you both something to eat.' Mother then looked at Father who was standing there looking like he was trying to figure it all out, that same look he had on his face

as we watched the fire in the town square on Monday evening.
'Do you know where that station is? I want you to go there and
see what's happening.' Mother said.

'Yes. I'm sure it's not far from here maybe only fifteen minutes
away. It's somewhere close to the slaughter house.' Father left
and Abigail and I went to the kitchen with Mother to have
something to eat. Hans came in and joined us with a big smile
on his face delighted with all the action in the house. He had
probably heard everything from the top of the stairs. He looked
at me with a cheeky grin on his face probably because I was
friends with a girl. I knew him so well and I always knew what
he was thinking.

'Do we know when we are supposed to go to the countryside?'
I asked Mother.

'No not yet Deiter, but we should be finding out soon enough.'
Mother replied. I sat looking out the window once again as I
always do, looking at the snow falling which as always was
helping me to go into a daydream. I hope we don't have to
leave soon I thought to myself. At least not until we find out
where Abigail's parents are. Not till we know what's going on
at the train station and if Abigail's parents have already gone to
the countryside. I just hope that whatever is going on that
Abigail can come to the countryside with us and that we get to
go on a train with seats, a train for people and not an animal
train. I sat and wondered where Father was and how he was
getting on looking for Abigail's Mother and Father. Everybody
talked away while I sat there daydreaming. We sat there for
over an hour until it was dark and Father still hadn't returned.
'If Father doesn't find your parents you can stay here tonight

Abigail. You can stay in the back bedroom and Hans you can stay in the front room with Deiter.' Mother said. That was such a relief because as it got dark I was starting to worry about what was going to happen to Abigail tonight. Hans looked to the heavens and wasn't looking too happy now about having to share a room with me again. The little cheeky grin was gone now from his face and had been replaced by a look of discontent which was a word Mother always used and I wasn't sure what it meant until she explained it to me. Abigail smiled and thanked Mother. That was the first time I'd seen her smile since we had been walking down the wide street this morning talking about the countryside and the fun we were going to have there.

Just then we heard dogs barking outside and men talking at the tops of their voices.

'Wait there.' Mother said. When Mother left the kitchen I got up and followed her. Mother walked quietly across the hall and into the shop. The shop light hadn't been turned on yet because when we left it was bright outside. The shop was dark but the street was bright with the reflection of the moon on the white snow lighting it up and also partially lighting up the inside of the shop. But it was still too dark for anybody out on the street to see in. Mother went to the window and I as far as the book shelves in the middle of the shop. We could both see that four or maybe five soldiers and two of those big brown and black dogs were on the street outside Abigail's house. They were banging on Abigail's front door so loudly and the dogs were barking so much that everybody on the street must have known they were there. I could see the curtains from other houses beside Abigail's were now moving and people were peeking out through to see what was happening. I whispered to Mother but she didn't know what I had said. She just looked back at me with a very cross look on her face. Even in this dark I knew it was a cross face because I had seen it many times before. Mothers cross face wasn't the one you had to really worry about as much as her angry face. Her angry face was worse than he cross face and if you seen Mother with an angry face you'd be better to run and hide. Her mouth always went to one side when she was angry. So far to one side that you would think she was trying to kiss her own earlobe. Probably the last time I had seen it was when Hans and I had eaten the eighteen squares of chocolate after everyone had gone to sleep and Mother the next morning had left Hans with the shape of a red hand on his face and his backside stinging. All I was trying to whisper to Mother was I hope nobody had seen Abigail come into our house.

Then without warning, a loud bang and a crashing sound when one of the soldiers kicked the front door of Abigail's house open. Some of the soldiers went inside and brought the two dogs inside with them. Two soldiers stood outside looking up and down the street waiting for the other soldiers to finish searching the house which is what I am guessing they were doing. But I can only guess because sometimes when you have nobody to ask what they think is happening, you have to guess. They must be searching for Abigail. Maybe they have just realised she is missing and should be with her parents. I know she wants to be with her parents but not today, not on those animal trains. I thought to myself I hope they don't come over here to search our house because those dogs can smell somebody from a mile away and would surely find Abigail even if we hid her behind the secret door in the shelves.

Mother and I stood in the book shop and watched and waited to see what was going to happen. The snow had stopped now and the street was as bright as day from the full moon that I could see in the sky just above Abigail's house. The soldiers came back out of the house, stood on the street talking for a few moments and then left, walking in the opposite direction away from the town square. Just then coming from the town square direction was Father. He came in the front door and for the first time ever there was no ringing sound from the bell which had been over the front door for as long as I can remember.

Mother whispered to Father telling him about the soldiers at Abigail's house. Father looked at me and said.

'Mother and I need to have a talk.' I understood that meant I was to leave the room. I didn't mind and went back into the kitchen where Hans and Abigail were talking and having a great laugh as if nothing was happening. Abigail asked.

'Who was outside making all that noise?' I think we had seen enough and worried enough for one day so I just said to Abigail.

'It was nothing just some strangers out for a walk because it's such a beautiful night.' Abigail looked a little happier now and not so worried anymore, so I just waited to see what Mother and Father would say now because they always knew best, well almost always knew best about most things but not everything because sometimes I think I knew better but enough about that for now. Hans and Abigail sat at the table talking away as if they'd known each other all their lives. Hans was like that he was never shy and could talk to anyone. I sat there thinking that we were going to have to hide Abigail now from the soldiers and that they would probably come back looking for her and searching all the houses on Bilker Street with those big brown and black dogs.

I still wondered what exactly was going on with the people who wore those yellow stars like Abigail and why did the soldiers not like them and why were they being sent away on the animal trains. Everything I thought about just confused me. I didn't understand much anymore about what was happening in Dusseldorf and probably all over Germany. Why were soldiers burning books and why were they shooting people. Where were Edward and Gustav gone and would we ever see them again. Would Abigail ever see her Mother or Father again. Nobody had any answers or maybe they did but they weren't going to tell me.

Mother came into the kitchen, while out in the shop we could hear Father locking the front door and hanging the bell back up, which was a good idea because at least with the bell ringing over the front door we'll know if someone is coming in.

Mother sat down at the table with us, looking very calm now and relaxed but still with a cross look on her face and in a very clear and calm voice she said.

'The soldiers are looking for Abigail tonight and probably tomorrow too because she was supposed to go with her parents today. We're not sure where they are gone but they probably went from the train station that you were at today. Everybody in Dusseldorf with that yellow star on their coats are being moved to a different part of the country but we think it would be much safer if Abigail stayed here with us.' Mother then paused for a couple of seconds and took a deep breath. Nobody spoke while we waited to see what she was to say next. Father then walked in and sat down.

'The soldiers are looking for a little girl and will keep looking for a little girl until they find her. So we thought it would be best Abigail, if you wore clothes belonging to the boys and a hat to cover your long hair. It would be best if you didn't go outside.
Father is going to the station to get train tickets tomorrow morning. We are going to Berlin at some time tomorrow but we're not sure yet what time. We're going there to Grandmothers house, but only for one day and we'll be coming back then and Grandmother will be coming with us. Grandmother was always going to come with us when they decided to evacuate the city. Abigail and Deiter can come with me and Father and Hans can stay here. Hopefully they will have given up looking for Abigail by the time we get back.'

Old people always use words that children just don't understand like evacuate, but they also came up with great plans that children could never think of. Hans looked at Abigail with a smile on his face and said. 'Grandmother is very funny and she forgets everything so she'll never be able to tell the soldiers about you.' Everybody looked at Hans and smiled. Then he said. 'She also smokes a pipe so the soldiers probably won't be able to see you through the big cloud of smoke.'

Everybody laughed. Hans could always think of something funny to say to make everyone laugh.

One time about a year ago at a funeral not far from where we live, everyone was feeling really sad, some were even crying. One lady was talking and said something about the old man in the Coffin. Hans looked up at everyone and said out loud.

'I didn't hear him coughing.' Everybody laughed even the people who were crying. Hans always said something to try and make people laugh. He pretended he didn't know what he was saying but he knew alright. It was as if sometimes he pretended to be a little silly so as he could say something silly and get away with it, just to make people laugh.

It was a great plan to travel to Berlin and another great adventure to look forward to. Although today's adventure didn't turn out to be great at all, it turned out to be more of a nightmare than an adventure. Maybe not all adventures are supposed to be happy ones, maybe some will just teach you a lesson and today's adventure certainly thought us a lesson about what was happening in Germany in order to make our country great again. I didn't understand everything about what was happening but I knew more now tonight than I did this morning even if I just couldn't figure it all out yet.

Father was going to buy three train tickets in the morning and we were going to travel to Berlin with Mother. Abigail was going to pretend to be Hans if anybody asked and I was to pretend to be myself. Pretending to be myself should be easy enough, pretending to be Hans for Abigail was going to be a different story and wasn't going to be easy but Mother said nobody should ask. When we get to Berlin nobody there would be looking for Abigail anymore. And maybe when we get to Berlin we might get to see or even meet the 'Fuhrer' the man that everybody seems to be talking about these days with the silly moustache. Maybe he might know where Edward and Gustav are. Although I don't think Mother likes him very much for some reason. So I don't think she'll want to meet him, but maybe we might or maybe Grandmother might know him and bring us to see him.

Chapter Seven

January 29th 1942
Day Four
Hiding behind the Secret Door

On this morning I woke up earlier than usual, earlier than if I were going to school or if it were just a normal day. I woke up earlier this morning probably because I was a little excited about going to Berlin and probably because Abigail was sleeping only maybe ten feet from where I was sleeping. I jumped out of bed and went straight to the window because that was a habit I was in now, and tried to look out. The window was frozen over but there was no need to see out this morning for I knew Abigail wasn't out there but this morning she was sleeping in our house. Hans was still asleep in bed and probably will be until Mother has to wake him. I got dressed as fast as I could in the middle of the floor. I wasn't bothered to get back into bed to get dressed because I'd probably only wake Hans. I quietly opened my door and went out across to Abigail's bedroom which used to be Hans bedroom and which used to be both our bedrooms before that when Edward and Gustav lived here. It was straight across from mine.
I slowly and very gently pushed the door open and looked inside. Abigail was gone, I turned and went straight for the

stairs and walked down the very steep steps taking one step at a time and listening to what was going on downstairs. I could hear Father talking to someone in the shop. It seemed very early for people to be in the shop. When I got to the bottom I walked on the last step which made such a loud creek that even the neighbours must have heard it. Well my Father heard it anyway. Just then I heard him call out.

'Hans is that you?' He paused. 'Deiter is it you?'
'It's me Father.' I replied.

I went straight into the shop. Father was standing at the front door talking to two soldiers while three more soldiers were outside the shop window with their brown and black dogs. The dogs were quite calm and looking at their reflections in the shop window as were the soldiers. Father was explaining to the soldiers that he hadn't seen the family or the little girl from across the street in a number of days or that he wouldn't really notice these things anyway because he was just too busy.

'Well we are going to have to come in and search your house Sir. We are going to search every house on the street.' The soldier said to Father.

'That's fine.' Father said. I was trying not to look worried in front of the soldiers but I don't think they were paying too much attention to me anyway. Also Father seemed to have everything under control. I wasn't even really sure where Abigail was. Maybe she had left with Mother earlier.

'You can all come in if you want and search the house but it won't take long because it's very small. We have no basement and no attic, only two rooms down stairs and a hall, three bedrooms upstairs and a small bathroom. Come in but leave those dogs outside. I don't want dogs coming into my shop. The last time a dog came in here he pulled books down off the shelves and tore some of them to shreds and made a terrible mess. I don't think you'll need dogs to search such a small house anyway.' The soldiers were very young and only seemed to be around the same age as Edward or Gustav. They seemed to me to be a little afraid of Father judging by the way they spoke to him.

'That's fine Sir it will only take a few minutes.' Two soldiers came in and each one walked around the book shelves in the middle of the floor in a different direction. They both wore their very smart looking uniforms but one of the soldier's wore a different coloured uniform than usual. I had never seen a soldier wearing what looked like all the other uniforms but his was all black and even looked smarter than the others. He also looked more important than the rest and meaner too. He was very tall with blond hair just like Hans and had really bright blue eyes. He never once smiled or looked like he was in any way friendly. He had a red scar on his face that went from the outside corner of his left eye in a curve downwards to the corner of his mouth. He walked with a limp and he moved a little slower than the other soldier.

They walked out into the hall and one went up the stairs and the other into the kitchen. Mother was in the kitchen and the soldier just said hello to her and left again in a matter of seconds and followed the other soldier up the stairs. I sat in the red chair and looked at Father who wasn't looking too worried but was still guarding the front door. I looked out the window at the other soldiers outside who also didn't look too worried or even that bothered about what was going on inside. They were too busy talking to each other and looking at themselves in the shop window.

Just then Hans arrived in and looked at Father, who looked back and slowly put his pointing finger up to his lips, pointing upwards and touching the bottom of his nose but didn't make any sound. Hans knew and I knew that was the sign to stay silent and not to say a word. The soldiers seemed to be upstairs for a very long time searching. All I could hear was rumbling sounds as they searched, rumbling sounds like what could be heard most nights when I was in bed. Rumbling sounds were the reason we would soon be going to the countryside. I was now guessing because Mother was in the kitchen that Abigail was behind the secret door. They would never find her in there as long as the dogs didn't come in. Mother now came into the shop and grabbed Hans by the hand and brought him into the kitchen for breakfast. Mother also seemed as if she wasn't very worried. I sat back in the big red chair and grabbed a book from the shelf and just relaxed and pretended to read it so as when the soldiers came back down I wouldn't look too worried. 'And Then There Were None. Agatha Christie.' I opened the book and started to read the first page. Strangely enough it started with a man on a train in the first class smoking carriage, and as I read on I just got bored and just pretended to read it. It was one of those books for grownups as most books were in Father's shop.

The soldiers came back down from upstairs and back into the shop and the soldier in the black uniform stopped, stood over me and looked at me sitting back in the red chair. He stood over me and looked straight into my eyes. He studied my face and said in a cross voice like Father would sometimes use.

'Have you seen the girl from across the street?' I looked up at him and thought to myself that I hadn't seen Abigail today so I wasn't really telling a lie.

'No Sir. I haven't seen her.' I said in a very relaxed voice while making sure to breath properly so as not to stammer.

'Do you know the girl from across the street?

Her name is Abigail Blaustein.'
'Not really sir, she doesn't go to our school and I've never really spoken to her in my life or even said hello. She has different friends than I do and plays different games, games that a boy would never play.'

He looked down at me for a couple of seconds but didn't speak. I think he was trying to figure out if I was telling a lie or not. The scar on his face was red and shining and his eyes that I thought were bright blue looked a little different when he was closer to me now. His right eye was bright blue and looked straight at me while his left eye the one with the scar beside it was blue but didn't look real at all and looked as if it wasn't looking at me but just doing its own thing and that he had no control over it. This made him look even more frightening than any of the other soldiers.

I'm glad he didn't tell me to hold my tongue out because everybody knew that if you told a lie that your tongue would turn black and mine must have been as black as the sky at night or even as black as his uniform or the boots he was wearing.

He turned and walked out through the front door thanking Father as he left. Father closed the front door and the bell gave a loud ring. Father and I went back towards the kitchen and as we left the shop Father whispered.

'Stay where you are Abigail.' Yes I was right Abigail was of course behind the secret door in Father's Office. We went to the Kitchen where Hans and Mother were waiting.

'I'm going to the station now to get three tickets for the train to Berlin, I'll know the train times when I get back and you can leave then.' Father said in a sort of whisper like somebody was listening. I guess that's how you must have to speak if you're a spy or when you're on a secret mission. Mother gave me some clothes and said. 'Give these to Abigail and tell her to put them on, just make sure nobody is looking through the window when you go into Father's office.' I went back through the hall and into the shop, took a look out through the window where there was only a few people walking up and down the street, but no soldiers. I pushed open the secret door to the office and went inside and closed it behind me. I got a shock when I seen Abigail was sitting on Fathers office chair with a gun in her hand that she had found in the table drawer.

'Look Deiter it's a real gun, I found it in the top drawer.'

I was a little surprised to see Abigail sitting back and pointing a gun in my direction. I knew there were no bullets in it because Father would never keep a loaded gun but I knew there were bullets somewhere. 'It looks like the guns the soldiers use. There are some bullets in the drawer too and I thought I was going to have to use it if the soldiers came in, does it work?'

Left page:

...hat has proper seats and tables and hopefully we will
...t in the countryside maybe next week.

...said.

...should just walk as fast as you can to the train station and
...t stop to speak to anyone. When you arrive the train
...ld be on the platform and you should be able to get on
...hout any questions being asked because you are only
...velling to Berlin and not going to another country.'

...e waited for around twenty minutes in the shop talking and
...ughing and Hans telling stories about Grandmother as loud
...s he could so Abigail could hear them too. Hans warned
...Abigail with a big grin on his face that Grandmother will keep
...asking the same question over and over again and that she will
...tell you the same story twice or maybe three times.

It's very strange how Grandmother can't remember what she
said just a few minutes before or what happened yesterday. But
she can tell you about everything that happened sixty years ago
or tell you everything about the day she got married to
Grandfather which she loves to do.
Grandmother always tells the story about the day Grandfather
went to fight in the first war but I don't like that story because
it's always very sad and Grandmother always cries when she's
telling you.

The same soldiers that searched the house this morning were
outside again at the house across the street next door to
Abigail's house. It was time for us to go to the station now as
we had thirty minutes left to get there. The tall blond soldier

Abigail asked.
'I think it does work, it used to belong to Grandfather before he
died. Put it back before Father comes in.' Abigail put the gun
back in the drawer, closed it gently and looked up at me and
asked.

'What time are we going to Berlin at today?'

Now so much was happening this morning and so much was
going through my head that I couldn't think of what to say to
Abigail about using a gun or shooting soldiers. I knew there
weren't enough bullets to shoot all the soldiers that would
come if she had shot the soldier in the black uniform or the few
soldiers and their dogs that were here this morning. But I just
thought to myself that she looked so funny sitting there behind
the office table thinking about taking on the whole German
army with one gun. I have only known her now for a few days
but I just wish we could run away forever away from all these
soldiers, away from Dusseldorf and even Berlin and just go
straight to the countryside today. I put the clothes on the table
and said. 'I'm not sure what time we're going yet, Father is
going to get tickets and Mother said you have to put these
clothes on so you might look more like a boy. I hope nobody
asks any questions and we get to go to Berlin safely to see
Grandmother.' Abigail looked at me and said. 'I hope this
adventure ends better than yesterday's adventure. I thought it
was already over when the soldiers came in this morning.'

'Not to worry Abigail, Father wouldn't let the soldiers bring the
dogs in so they could never find you and I'm sure today's
adventure will end better than yesterday because at least today
we'll be going to the proper train station.' I heard the shop door

bell ring and I turned a little worried that the soldiers were back. I peeked through the shelves into the shop and could see Father walking outside past the shop window. I told Abigail it was only Father which as I could see by her face was a great relief. I thought of how worried Abigail must have been when the soldiers were in the shop and upstairs searching for her and I understood why she might want to use a gun to protect herself especially after everything we had seen the day before at the train station.

'I'm going to the kitchen now so you can get dressed and I'll bring you back some breakfast in a few minutes. Father said you are to stay in here until we're going to the station just in case the soldiers come back.'

I opened the door and as I was leaving Abigail stood up and walked towards me and once again just as before in exactly the same place standing just inside the secret door, she kissed me on the cheek. I walked back to the kitchen, my face red and my heart beating at one hundred miles per hour, thinking of everything and with this race horse running in my head again. Why didn't I kiss her back? Why did she kiss me this time? It felt different than the last time. Was she only kissing me because she was thankful that we were helping her? It felt as if we were boyfriend and girlfriend the last time but this time I don't know what it meant and I was never going to ask. I had so much to think of and so much to worry about. Maybe I should just stop thinking so much about everything, stop thinking and worrying about what was happening and just be happy that Abigail had just kissed me.

Chapter Eig

Travelling to Be

The shop door bell rang again and it was Father. It h him about an hour to get there and back. He told us h bought three train tickets to Berlin for the next train w in about one hour. It was only going to take us twenty n to get to the station and Mother already knew the way. A was still hiding behind the secret door when Father came but she could hear everything we were saying.

'The streets are full with soldiers between here and the statior Father said.

'The soldiers are searching the houses but they're not just searching for Abigail.'

'Who are they searching for?' I asked.

'I'm not really sure but maybe Abigail isn't the only one to go missing or get lost.' I thought this was strange because Abigail hasn't gone missing or gotten lost. She is here with us and just missed her parents when they were going to the station to get a train to the countryside. But I'd say Abigail is glad she did miss them because they ended up going on one of those Animal trains and all because Abigail's Mother and Father wore a patch on their clothes of a yellow star. But now if Abigail comes to the countryside with us she will get to go on a train for people and

Abigail asked.

'I think it does work, it used to belong to Grandfather before he died. Put it back before Father comes in.' Abigail put the gun back in the drawer, closed it gently and looked up at me and asked.

'What time are we going to Berlin at today?'

Now so much was happening this morning and so much was going through my head that I couldn't think of what to say to Abigail about using a gun or shooting soldiers. I knew there weren't enough bullets to shoot all the soldiers that would come if she had shot the soldier in the black uniform or the few soldiers and their dogs that were here this morning. But I just thought to myself that she looked so funny sitting there behind the office table thinking about taking on the whole German army with one gun. I have only known her now for a few days but I just wish we could run away forever away from all these soldiers, away from Dusseldorf and even Berlin and just go straight to the countryside today. I put the clothes on the table and said. 'I'm not sure what time we're going yet, Father is going to get tickets and Mother said you have to put these clothes on so you might look more like a boy. I hope nobody asks any questions and we get to go to Berlin safely to see Grandmother.' Abigail looked at me and said. 'I hope this adventure ends better than yesterday's adventure. I thought it was already over when the soldiers came in this morning.'

'Not to worry Abigail, Father wouldn't let the soldiers bring the dogs in so they could never find you and I'm sure today's adventure will end better than yesterday because at least today we'll be going to the proper train station.' I heard the shop door bell ring and I turned a little worried that the soldiers were back. I peeked through the shelves into the shop and could see Father walking outside past the shop window. I told Abigail it was only Father which as I could see by her face was a great relief. I thought of how worried Abigail must have been when the soldiers were in the shop and upstairs searching for her and I understood why she might want to use a gun to protect herself especially after everything we had seen the day before at the train station.

'I'm going to the kitchen now so you can get dressed and I'll bring you back some breakfast in a few minutes. Father said you are to stay in here until we're going to the station just in case the soldiers come back.'

I opened the door and as I was leaving Abigail stood up and walked towards me and once again just as before in exactly the same place standing just inside the secret door, she kissed me on the cheek. I walked back to the kitchen, my face red and my heart beating at one hundred miles per hour, thinking of everything and with this race horse running in my head again. Why didn't I kiss her back? Why did she kiss me this time? It felt different than the last time. Was she only kissing me because she was thankful that we were helping her? It felt as if we were boyfriend and girlfriend the last time but this time I don't know what it meant and I was never going to ask. I had so much to think of and so much to worry about. Maybe I should just stop thinking so much about everything, stop thinking and worrying about what was happening and just be happy that Abigail had just kissed me.

Chapter Eight

Travelling to Berlin

The shop door bell rang again and it was Father. It had taken him about an hour to get there and back. He told us he had bought three train tickets to Berlin for the next train which left in about one hour. It was only going to take us twenty minutes to get to the station and Mother already knew the way. Abigail was still hiding behind the secret door when Father came in, but she could hear everything we were saying.

'The streets are full with soldiers between here and the station.' Father said.

'The soldiers are searching the houses but they're not just searching for Abigail.'

'Who are they searching for?' I asked.

'I'm not really sure but maybe Abigail isn't the only one to go missing or get lost.' I thought this was strange because Abigail hasn't gone missing or gotten lost. She is here with us and just missed her parents when they were going to the station to get a train to the countryside. But I'd say Abigail is glad she did miss them because they ended up going on one of those Animal trains and all because Abigail's Mother and Father wore a patch on their clothes of a yellow star. But now if Abigail comes to the countryside with us she will get to go on a train for people and a train that has proper seats and tables and hopefully we will all meet in the countryside maybe next week.

Father said.

'You should just walk as fast as you can to the train station and don't stop to speak to anyone. When you arrive the train should be on the platform and you should be able to get on without any questions being asked because you are only travelling to Berlin and not going to another country.'

We waited for around twenty minutes in the shop talking and laughing and Hans telling stories about Grandmother as loud as he could so Abigail could hear them too. Hans warned Abigail with a big grin on his face that Grandmother will keep asking the same question over and over again and that she will tell you the same story twice or maybe three times.

It's very strange how Grandmother can't remember what she said just a few minutes before or what happened yesterday. But she can tell you about everything that happened sixty years ago or tell you everything about the day she got married to Grandfather which she loves to do.
Grandmother always tells the story about the day Grandfather went to fight in the first war but I don't like that story because it's always very sad and Grandmother always cries when she's telling you.

The same soldiers that searched the house this morning were outside again at the house across the street next door to Abigail's house. It was time for us to go to the station now as we had thirty minutes left to get there. The tall blond soldier with the scar on his face in the black uniform that stopped to ask me questions this morning was now looking back across at our house. Father told Hans to go to the kitchen while he went out to speak to the soldiers. While he was speaking to the soldiers and got their backs turned we were to leave and walk as quickly as we could in the opposite direction to the train station. Father went outside and slowly walked over to the group of soldiers. It would have been better if it was snowing because the soldiers might not be out or would have less chance of seeing us, but the sun was actually shining at the moment which was strange these days. I stood at the secret door looking out the window waiting for Father to give us a signal. Mother said time was running out. Just then we noticed the soldiers all had their backs turned looking down the street in the opposite direction at whatever Father was pointing at. I pushed the secret door open and Abigail came out dressed in clothes that made her look just like myself or Hans and wearing a hat with her hair up underneath it.

We all walked to the front door but when Mother opened the door the bell rang loud enough for everyone to hear. The soldiers and Father all turned and looked at us. We walked out the door and kept going and the door closed behind us with a loud ring once again. We walked away down the street knowing the soldiers were all watching us. I could hear Father say to the soldiers that Mother was bringing the boys for a walk to the town square while the sun was shining. I was shaking with nerves and feeling a little sick from worrying that the mean soldier in the black uniform might follow us. I carried my bag over my shoulder which was heavier than it should be because Hans had given me a present all wrapped up for

Grandmother. We never looked back over our shoulders once to see if they were still watching, we just kept walking till we were out of sight. We arrived at the old town square with the statue of the horse with a man on his back and where they had the fire of nothing only books. We walked through the square passed the statue and the town hall, and out of the square and down a different street than Abigail and I took to the station yesterday. The old lady had given us the wrong directions which led us to the wrong station. But now thinking about it as we walked out of the square maybe it was the best thing because now we knew about the other station and the animal trains that Abigail could have ended up going on. It didn't take us long till we arrived at the proper station. Over the station entrance was a large sign that read.

'HAUPTBAHNHOF TRAIN STATION.'

I was so relieved to see that this was a real train station with proper trains that people could travel on. There were no soldiers here with those big brown and black dogs standing outside or I couldn't see one train that would be used for animals. The station was really busy with what looked like hundreds of people standing waiting for their trains or people walking around like they were lost or were looking for something they had misplaced. Men were queuing for tickets while their families stood back and waited. Everybody was busy rushing about and nobody looked like they had a second to stop or talk. I couldn't see any soldiers here inside the station or on the platform so it looked like we might already be safe. Mother asked somebody who looked like they worked at the station where the train to Berlin was. He pointed us towards what looked like a beautiful new train and we already had our tickets so we went straight over. The step up onto the train was quite high and there was a gap between the train and platform that led under the train which didn't look like a place you would want to end up. You couldn't really see down there with the steam and smoke but it made me feel a little nervous that I might fall in. I thought I better make sure to be careful when climbing on board. Abigail climbed up the step and onto the train first, then Mother gave me a lift up onto the step and I went inside and then Mother climbed on board last. We got three seats together with Abigail and I sitting beside each other and Mother sat across from us on the other side of the table. Mother faced in the direction that the train was travelling because she said she would feel sick travelling backwards if she faced in the other direction. I thought this was a bit strange but I hoped I wouldn't feel sick travelling backwards and I hoped I wouldn't have to move because I was quite happy sitting beside Abigail. The train pulled out of the station about ten minutes late and Mother just said that was normal. Trains were never on time when leaving or arriving.

Father had given me his Ruhla pocket watch and chain before we left for the trip to Berlin and told me to keep it with me at all times and to make sure not to lose it as he had gotten it from his Father. I could use it for a few days so as we wouldn't be late for anything he said. Not for as long as I can remember have I ever seen Father without his pocket watch and chain. It was the only thing he had belonging to his Father. Father said I had to wind it every day and that I could set the correct time by checking different clocks that I passed on my journey. I had just set it to the correct time by the clock tower at the train station before we left. I showed Abigail the watch and she said she had never seen anything so nice before and she thought that maybe someday Father would give the watch to me and then I would give it to my son and so on. We were now outside Dusseldorf and flying through the countryside and small towns along the way which we could see in the distance. The snow was falling again heavier than normal or at least it looked like it was falling heavier but maybe it was the speed that the train was travelling at. Everywhere along the way looked the same colour as our town. The whole world just looked grey and white. But here in the countryside not a sign of a red and white flag to add a splash of colour to the world. I looked out at the snow falling sideways passed my window faster than ever I had seen snow fall before and the sound of the train moving like the rhythm or beat of a song and then I could feel myself getting sleepy and then that was the last thing I could remember. Later I woke up feeling a little strange and for a second trying to figure out where I was. It didn't take long to remember because the sounds and view were the same as before I had fallen asleep but now it was dark outside.

Abigail and Mother were asleep too and I was a little confused as to how much time had passed. I checked Fathers watch and much to my surprise over three hours had passed in what seemed just like a couple of seconds. The train was warm and just about everyone on our carriage was asleep. Everybody including Abigail and Mother were rocking from side to side as the train moved. Some had their heads against the windows and their heads just rolled and moved from side to side on the glass. From time to time someone might wake when their head moved too fast or shook too hard but they would put their head back to the glass and fall asleep again. One man tried to sleep sitting upwards but every time his head fell forward he woke up and sat back up straight and fell back asleep again only to do the same thing all over again. The snow had stopped and as I looked out the window of the train there seemed to be more lights up in the sky than on the ground. The sky looked to be full of stars and what looked like the lights from planes flying over. There were bright flashing lights coming out of the ground and were flying up in the direction of the planes. Then I could see what seemed to be a ball of light falling, which looked like fire falling from the sky. It looked very strange and I'm not sure what was happening and I couldn't wake Mother to ask her.

Thankfully it started to get brighter outside, brighter from the lights of a city or town. I sat there hoping this was Berlin because I was getting bored with nobody to talk to and nothing to do. The only good thing now was Abigail had her head on the side of my arm close to my shoulder as she slept. I was her pillow which just made me feel so happy and gave me a little tingle in my heart. It wasn't very noticeable but I could feel the train slowing down now, the rhythm of the train was getting slower and one by one everybody on our carriage was waking up including Mother and Abigail.

'Have we arrived?' Abigail asked.
'I think so.' I replied.
'Will Grandmother be at the station in Berlin?'

I asked Mother.
'No it's too dark and cold for Grandmother to be out. We will get a tram to her house when we arrive.' The train stopped at

the station and I looked out the window and could see on the platform a sign that read.

'BERLIN ANHALTER BAHNHOF.'

Once I could see the word Berlin I was satisfied that we had arrived. The station was as busy as the station in Dusseldorf with people rushing around and nobody stopping to talk or even say hello to each other. We got up and walked towards the door but had to wait for a minute in a queue to get off the train. One old lady rubbed Abigail on the head and said to Mother.

'They're two very pretty little boys you have there.'

'Thank you.' Mother said. Abigail and I smiled at each other because it was funny that someone thought she was a boy and I was happy to think that at least our plan was working and someone actually did think she was a boy. But now that we were in Berlin we probably didn't have to worry about that anymore because the tall soldier with the blond hair and black uniform wasn't around. We got off the train and walked down the platform towards the exit very slowly due to the crowds of people on the platform now. I noticed that there were a lot of soldiers on the station platform but thankfully they didn't have their dogs with them. On another platform I could see lots of families getting onto a train and they all had the yellow star patches on their clothes. They were all boarding a proper train with seats and not like in Dusseldorf where they were going to the countryside on animal trains. I pointed over to show Abigail, she looked for a while and then looked back at me a shrugged her shoulders. This was very strange just like almost everything I see these days. Just like the planes and the flashing lights coming out of the ground I could see on the way here and that was another thing to add to a list of strange things happening in Germany these days. Walking up the platform I could feel a freezing cold wind blowing in my face. It seemed to be colder here in Berlin than it was in Dusseldorf or maybe it just feels like that when you're in a strange place.

We left the station and were now standing in a freezing blustery snow storm on a large and very wide cobble stone street with trams moving up and down in both directions. There were swarms of mostly grownups walking in all directions with their heads down avoiding the snow and freezing wind. Mother held both our hands like she would Hans and I. She never spoke but she moved like everyone else as if she knew where she was going. We stopped in the middle of the wide street and I looked up and I could see a tram coming in our direction. The tram stopped and Mother lifted us on board wasting no time because everybody in Berlin was in a hurry tonight. The tram moved at a nice pace along the street but not as fast as the train moved through the countryside and for the moment it felt warmer because we were in out of the freezing wind. Berlin just like Dusseldorf had those red flags hanging from every building and they were even bigger than the ones in Dusseldorf. They seemed to have flags in every shape hanging even some the full length of the buildings and not just the normal ones like at home.

The tram stopped and Mother jumped up and said. 'This is us.' We jumped down from the tram and stood to one side as it pulled away. Mother looked in both directions up and down the street and then grabbed both our hands again without

saying a word and we started walking. It was just so cold that it
was hard to talk and no matter how fast we walked I couldn't
feel myself getting any warmer. My teeth were now starting to
rattle and my toes were so numb that they felt like they weren't
even there anymore. Then we arrived at a small street much
like Bilker Street and stopped outside a house and Mother
knocked at the door. The door opened and Grandmother stood
just inside the door in a cloud of smoke squinting out at us and
scratching the back of her head while puffing on her pipe.

'Who's that?'
'It's me Mama! It's me your daughter Sofia.' Mother said.
'Come in, come in at once.' Grandmother replied. We went
inside and before we even got a chance to take our coats off and
sit down the questions started just like Hans said they would.

'How did you get here?' Grandmother asked.

'On the train and we took the tram up to the house because it
was just too far to walk in the cold.'

'That was an excellent idea.' Grandmother replied as if
sounding a bit cheeky the way Hans might say things
sometimes and then she asked.

'Do the horses still pull the trams?'

'I don't think so, I didn't notice any horses.' I said a little
confused and looking at Mother to see if I was right or were
there actually horses and I was too cold to notice them.

'Well it was much better when the horses did pull the trams.'
Grandmother said sounding a bit cross.

'Who are these two lovely little boys?'
'This is your Grandson Deiter and our friend Abigail.'
Grandmother looked at us and said. 'Now why would
somebody call a boy Abigail? Sure isn't that a girl's name?' We
all smiled and looked at Abigail who was blushing a little now.
'No Grandmother, Abigail is a girl.'

I was going to start explaining the story and why Abigail was
dressed like a boy but it was just too much and it would only
confuse Grandmother even more. I'm not sure she was even
fully sure who we were. She stood for a while puffing on her
pipe and looking at us smiling.

'Did it take long to get here?'

'Not long, only maybe a few hours.' Mother said. Grandmother
smiled.

'Good good and how did you get here?' 'On the train and then
we took the tram.' 'Oh very good, do the horses still pull the
trams?' 'No not any more mama but it was better when they
did.' Mother replied.

Mother called Grandmother Mama which sounded strange to
me to hear my Mother call someone Mama.

'Yes it sure was, the horses did a much better job.' Silence for a
few seconds, I knew what was coming next.

'And who are these two lovely little boys.' 'This is your
grandson Deiter and the girl from across the street, Abigail.'
'That's a lovely name for a girl.'
'Did it take you long to get here?'

'Not long.'

We all sat down in the front room of the house which was really dark and only lit by two candles. Grandmother sat in what I would guess was her favourite chair beside the window where she could see out onto the street. She kept one eye on the street at all times and still sat back and smoked her pipe and talked to us. Her favourite thing to talk about was the war. The first war that is, the war that Grandfather died in and she always said that all he left behind was his pipe. She said she was still smoking it because it reminded her of him.

It had a really strong smell which was really nice and I would think that a smell that strong would easily remind you of somebody. Smells could always bring back a memory or remind you of something. Sometimes a memory that you couldn't even properly remember but you knew it happened like when you wake from a dream and forget your dream straight away. It's always there at the back of your mind waiting to come back again. It's there but you're not sure if it even happened. And sometimes a strong smell will bring it back to you again. Whether it is flowers or smoke, the smell of soap or certain foods or the smell of a cold morning, smells could always remind you of something or somebody.

Just then I remembered that Hans had given me a present for grandmother that was in my bag that I had carried all the way from Dusseldorf. I didn't know what the present was but he had it wrapped in a brown paper bag belonging to the shop, a bag that was for putting books into. It was tied up with string and no one was to open it only grandmother. The present had doubled or even tripled the weight of my bag and left my arm sore and tired any time I had to carry it and it left my shoulder nearly bruised when I carried my bag over my shoulder. I gave it to grandmother and she opened it and looked into the bag. I knew by the smile on her face that she was happy with what was wrapped up in the bag. Mother asked. 'What is it, can we have a look?' Grandmother took a huge cobble stone out of the bag and held it up with her two hands in front of us with a big smile on her face. A huge cobble stone I thought to myself. Why? Why would Hans make me carry a cobble stone all the way from Dusseldorf to Berlin when they've got millions of cobble stones in Berlin already? We have stacks of them in our back garden and Grandmother probably has stacks of them in her back garden too. I thought of how sore and tired my shoulder and arms were carrying it here and I wondered what Hans was thinking. Just then Grandmother took a note out of the bag and held it up in the air.

'What does it say?' Mother asked. Grandmother opened the folded note and read it out loud.

'Hope you like it Grandmother and don't forget to thank Deiter for bringing it all the way from Dusseldorf.' Everybody laughed except me. I thought about it for another few seconds while everyone was laughing and finally it dawned on me that Hans was joking when he made me carry it in my bag all the way here to Berlin from Dusseldorf. And the joke was on me. Then I had to join in and laugh with everyone else even though I still wasn't finding it very funny. I knew that Hans would just find this hilarious and would be back in Dusseldorf now having a good laugh and wishing he was here to see the look on my face when I realised what was in the bag. Hans was always doing things like this for a laugh and that I didn't find very funny but after time passed and the more everyone talked about it the more it would sink in, I would start to get the joke. I looked around the room and everyone was so happy and laughing at the way Grandmother was holding the stone up in the air like she had just won a trophy and with the pipe hanging from her mouth she looked like a chimney with the smoke rising up in the air and past the stone and up to the ceiling. It really was starting to get funnier already.

It was getting very late now and I knew it was nearly time to go to bed and that Mother any minute now would be saying. 'Off to bed with you now you have to be up early in the morning.' Mother always said that even when we didn't have to be up early in the morning. I didn't feel very tired as I had slept for at least three hours on the train. But I thought the best thing to do was to go to bed as a lot of things were rushing around inside my head that had happened today. From the trains at the station and the planes in the sky and Abigail behind the secret door while the soldier in the black uniform looked at me with his weird eyes and asked me questions. I took out Fathers watch and set it by the clock in the room. Grandmother then got very excited and said.

'Tomorrow we are going to the Berlin Sportpalast to see The Fuhrer Adolf Hitler.' She said he was a great man and was going to make this a great country again. Mother didn't look very happy about this. I don't think she really liked The Fuhrer.

'We'll see mama, we might be too busy.' I couldn't see how we'd be too busy as we were here just to see Grandmother and to bring her back to Dusseldorf with us and we didn't have anything else to do. Grandmother looked out the window for a while and then turned to us looking really excited and said.

98

'We are going to the Berlin Sportpalast to see The Fuhrer Adolf....' Mother interrupted and just said. 'That's fine mama we know.' I closed my eyes even though I wasn't tired and sat back in the chair and listened to everyone talking and thought to myself that this was something to look forward to, as I had never before seen The Fuhrer.

Chapter Nine

January 30th 1942

Day Five

The Fuhrer's great speech

When I woke up I was in bed and I couldn't even remember going to bed or walking up the stairs or taking my clothes off. This was always happening to me and I always wondered when I woke first thing in the morning how did I get here but usually by the time I got downstairs and into the kitchen so much had went through my head that I would forget to ask.

I was so cold that I couldn't even lift the blankets to get my clothes so as to get dressed in the bed. I looked at my clothes folded nicely on the floor and was so sorry that somebody had even taken them off me because I would probably have left them on. The window in the room was frozen over and I couldn't see if it was snowing outside or not. I'm not sure if it is colder here in Berlin or is it that Grandmothers house is colder or both. My toes like last night are numb and probably have been now for the last few months. I just can't wait for the summer to come when we can play in the fields and rivers at the countryside. I know Hans, Abigail and I are going to have so much fun. I don't think I got very much sleep last night or maybe I did and I was actually dreaming when I heard the sounds of planes flying over and the rumbling sounds in the distance. I think Berlin might sound a lot like Dusseldorf at night only it might be louder here. Mother told us last night that like Dusseldorf they are at the moment evacuating all the children out of Berlin to the countryside. She said that there was a train full with children at the station when we arrived yesterday evening and they were all carrying little flags and waving them out the windows of the train. She said they all looked very happy to be going away. The only train I noticed last night was the train with the people getting on with the patches on their clothes of a yellow star and they weren't waving any flags. I never noticed any other train but I suppose I had my head down trying not to let the freezing cold wind at my face.

I jumped out of bed and grabbed my clothes and jumped straight back in again and got dressed under the blankets. I wondered was Abigail awake yet and was she looking forward to seeing The Fuhrer today. I wondered would she dress as a boy or a girl now that we had left Dusseldorf and the soldier in the black uniform couldn't find her here. I wasn't sure if Mother had brought Abigail's white dress in her suitcase or left it behind. Abigail hadn't got any other clothes and she had left her only coat in the lookout tower at the freight station. I don't think she would ever wear that coat again anyway unless of course she took off the patch of the yellow star first.

I jumped out of bed and went to the window to see if I could see anything outside but the window was totally frozen over and I didn't feel like trying to clear the frost on the glass this

101

morning. I could smell grandmother's pipe from here in my room so I knew she was up. I went straight down the stairs and as I reached the bottom step I hesitated for just a second and then skipped over it. I walked into the back room which like our house was the kitchen. Grandmother was sitting at the kitchen table and looking at a large piece of paper. I slowly walked over to her for I wasn't sure if she knew who I was. She turned and said.

'Good morning Deiter. Sit down there and take a look at that piece of paper.'

I looked at it and it had all the information about today's event at the sportpalast. At the top and in large writing it read. 'The Fuhrer Adolf Hitler' and it went on to say he would be at the sportpalast today. It had times and dates and it went on and on with a lot of words that I didn't really understand and those words that only the grownups used that most children didn't know or hadn't learned about in school yet.

'We'll be walking there today Deiter and we'll have to go early or we might not get in. If those other two don't get out of bed soon we'll have to just leave without them. This is too important to miss.'

Grandmother really seemed to like The Fuhrer a lot more than Mother or Father or anyone I knew. I hope that I might get a chance today to talk to The Fuhrer and maybe ask him about Edward and Gustav and if he might know where they are because after all they did join his army. Just then Abigail appeared and still dressed like a boy. I didn't mind and didn't say anything as I knew she had no other clothes. I don't think it mattered what Abigail wore she always looked beautiful anyway. I told Abigail we would be going to see The Fuhrer this morning with Grandmother. We sat down and had breakfast and laughed quietly as Grandmother asked the same questions over and over. We never really minded and answered without fail every time.

I went back up the stairs and into mother's room. Mother was still in bed and said she'd be getting up in a few minutes even though she said she was feeling a bit sick now.

'One thing is for sure.' Mother said.

'I will not be going to the sportpalast today.' I don't think she could even say the name The Fuhrer or Adolf Hitler.

'But can Abigail and I go to the sportpalast?'

'You can go if you want but stay close to Grandmother and don't let her out of your sight. Anyway Deiter I don't think you'll be able to understand a word of what that man is saying.'

I think mother could be right if the piece of paper downstairs is anything to go by. Mother gave me a kiss on my cheek just before I left to go back downstairs and before I even left her room I think she had fallen asleep.

Later as we were leaving Grandmother, Abigail and I shouted up the stairs at Mother to say goodbye and we left the house all really excited to go to the sportpalast. We walked down the street that we came up last night towards the tram line. I turned and asked grandmother. 'Do we walk there or go on the tram? Do you know which direction we have to go or what street it's on?' Grandmother looked at me and asked me something about the trams and the horses again. I think when Mother said we were to keep an eye on Grandmother it was so that she wouldn't get lost and not us. Grandmother hadn't a clue as to how we were going to get there she only knew where she wanted to go.

'Abigail I think this is going to be like our adventure to the train station. We are going to have to ask somebody for directions again.'

We spotted two old ladies standing talking and we approached them to ask for directions. They were the only people we could see that weren't rushing about and it's always safer to ask old people for directions.

'Excuse me but could you tell us how to get to the sportpalast?' I asked.

'Wait here with us now and the next tram to arrive here should be the right one to get us all to where we're going.'

Now I wasn't sure about these two old ladies or if they like Grandmother were just a little lost too. The ground was covered in a heavy blanket of snow from last night's snow storm and the tracks weren't visible on any of the streets. It was hard to tell what streets the trams were going to be travelling on and maybe we were standing in the middle of nowhere with a group of old folks waiting for a tram that was never going to arrive.

Just then the crowd on the street started to get bigger and more and more people were standing beside us now. I really hoped that a tram would arrive shortly or were all these crowds joining us thinking we knew there was a tram coming when really we were only two children and three very old ladies standing there not knowing what we were at. A few people were carrying small red flags with the white circle and strange black sign in the middle. One old lady smiled down at me and handed me two flags and I handed one to Abigail. Abigail shrugged her shoulders and smiled back at me and said thanks. I don't know everything about what is going on in Germany and the world today but I do know for some reason maybe it's just a feeling but I think it's better to be waving one of these red flags at the moment than it is to be wearing one of those patches of the yellow star and I don't know why that is, it just is.

Just then a tram came down the street heading straight towards us and we all had to jump back as we were actually standing on the tracks. Looks like all these old people knew what they were talking about after all. We all climbed on board and then it moved off nice and slowly and through the streets of Berlin.

I think everyone that got on was going to the sportpalast as they were all carrying flags like the ones we got from the old lady. We managed to get seats when we got on the tram and we were now sitting back enjoying the view as we slowly moved along the tracks through the city. Every street we went along had the red flags hanging up and they looked very well as they gave every building a nice splash of colour. Without them the streets would be just light grey and dark grey and everything covered in white snow. We then passed through a part of the city that looked to me like it could have been from a nightmare where all the buildings were falling down or completely levelled to the ground. Some still had fires burning inside them and others were just a pile of bricks and stones, timber and old slates that were piled higher than the tram. I could see a building that looked as if something had taken a perfect semi circular bite out of the roof and another that looked like one side of it had been stolen, or it had been chopped in half and you could look into it from the side at all the rooms. Even on the top floor you could see the inside of the rooms, the fireplaces, the table and chairs in the middle of the floor and the paint on the walls and the curtains on the windows and bedrooms with the beds still in the corner. I've never seen anything like this before and I could not think or even understand why anybody would do this to our city where so many people lived.

Now I knew why we had to move to the countryside and now I knew what the rumbling was at night time and all caused by those planes flying over. I knew but I didn't know why or couldn't even begin to understand why somebody from another country was flying planes over us at night and doing this to our beautiful city. Everyone on the tram was silent and just staring in amazement at the buildings that were knocked and the ones that were chopped in half.

One old lady on the tram told everybody that in London England they have trains and trams that travel in tunnels really deep under the ground. She said during the air raids people can go down there for safety from our bombers. Now I don't know how she knows this but I thought to myself that if we are flying planes over them and that means that they are probably the ones flying the planes over us and I thought why? None of this makes any sense what so ever that we are doing this to their city and they're doing it to ours. None of this is going to make our country great again. Then after a few more minutes we were back into a part of the city that looked perfect again with perfect grey buildings with perfect windows and doors and people walking around happy like as if the other part of the city didn't exist.

The tram then made its way down a very busy street before it stopped outside a large building. The crowds of people were all going in the one direction towards what I was now guessing was the sportspalast. We stepped down off the tram and Abigail and I held hands and followed Grandmother towards the building. I could see a large sign now up really high that read sportspalast and it was one of the largest buildings I'd ever seen with what looked like at least forty windows on the front and three large arched front doors.

It was surrounded by hundreds of soldiers all watching the crowds as they walked in through the front of the building. Thankfully the soldiers didn't have those brown and black dogs with them like they did outside the freight station in Dusseldorf. Everybody seemed very happy to be here and even I was starting to get excited and a little nervous now about seeing The Fuhrer.

We managed to get inside without having to wait around for very long as the crowd moved swiftly through the three front doors. We weren't very near the front but I think we were lucky to get inside as the doors closed just after we'd found three seats to sit down. Grandmother sat on the outside seat nearest the aisle while I sat on the third seat in and Abigail in the middle between us. A very large man came in and sat beside me. Mother said I wasn't to call somebody fat because it was bad manners but this man was really fat. I had to push closer to Abigail because he was taking up half my seat and probably half the seat on the other side of him as well. He smelled really terrible too and I couldn't believe that of all the seats in the sportspalast I had to end up sitting beside him. Then he decided to put his hand on my right leg for no reason and just leave it there. I remembered how Abigail had told me while we were walking to the freight station in Dusseldorf on our adventure that ended up being a nightmare, where the animal trains were, that she had an uncle who was always putting his hand on her leg or back or arm or somewhere while smiling at her. I told her that I had an uncle like this too and we agreed that maybe everyone in the world had an uncle like this that was just a little bit strange. Abigail could see the man's hand on my leg and she turned to me and whispered in my ear that maybe he was hungry and that my leg looked like a leg of chicken. We both laughed so loud that Grandmother turned and looked at us when we did. Then grandmother stood up and asked me to switch places with her. I moved and sat in her seat and she sat in mine beside the very large man. A couple of minutes later I leaned forward and looked and I noticed that he didn't have his hand on Grandmother's leg. I whispered in Abigail's ear that he mustn't be very hungry anymore. We both laughed again but not as loudly this time. We were very near the back but still had a view of where The Fuhrer was to make his speech from. Those red flags were hanging everywhere and there were all sorts of what I could only explain as statues of eagles with the strange funny shaped sign below them. I don't think I have seen so many people in one building before. Some of the crowd were so high up on balconies they could touch the ceiling and I wished we had gotten seats up there just to see what it would be like to look down on so many people. The front balcony facing back towards us was full with soldiers in all kinds of different types of really smart uniforms. Some of which were black uniforms just like the blond soldier was wearing back in Dusseldorf, the soldier that was looking for Abigail. I whispered to Abigail that I hoped he wasn't sitting up the front looking out into the crowd and could see us sitting here.

We sat for what seemed like at least an hour before anybody made any movement at the front where the soldiers sat. Everybody in the crowd sat talking and it just sounded like one big buzzing sound. Abigail and I sat and whispered about everything that had happened over the past few days and the train journey here and our trip back home tomorrow with Mother and Grandmother to Dusseldorf. The buzzing sound stopped and changed to loud cheering as The Fuhrer appeared on the platform at the front and the crowds stood up and clapped and cheered and waved flags with great excitement to see him. I couldn't believe that there he was, Adolf Hitler standing just in front of my eyes. Finally the crowd fell silent and The Fuhrer started to speak. There was complete silence as he spoke and I don't think anyone would dare talk now or even move in their seats.

When The Fuhrer started to speak I realised that mother was right and that this was not a speech for children as most of the words he used I just didn't understand. Most of the words were words used by grownups that children could never understand. Words that were to be seen in the books in Fathers shop that I often tried to read but usually gave up on after a few pages because I didn't know what was happening.

The Fuhrer spoke of Democracy which I heard about in school and I don't think he liked it very much and Chamberlain who I'm guessing was a man which he didn't like very much either and won't be calling around to his house any time soon. We sat in amazement at how loudly he spoke and how much he waved his hands in the air to express how he felt and at how much the crowd loved him and agreed with everything he said. I couldn't agree or disagree because most of what he talked about I didn't understand and it just confused me. I understood things he said like our great nation and our enemies. Other words I tried to memorise so as I could try to find out later what they meant were words like resurrection, danger of extinction, conscription, economic prosperity and economic destitution but I have a feeling I will never know what they mean.

The Fuhrer talked about the treaty of Versailles which I have heard before but not sure exactly what it is and he spoke of peace with Russia and World war. I understood words I have heard before like Luftwaffe and the Navy, Wehrmacht and the Army, Poland, The British Empire and the U boats. But he spoke for so long and said so much that, that is just about all I can really remember of what he said. I know that whatever he was talking about all that time must have been really great because the crowd cheered and waved their flags when he finished in a way that really proved they loved him and that he must be a great man or maybe one of the greatest men in the world.

Abigail and I waved our flags and cheered like we loved him too even though we didn't understand what he was talking about. And I still don't understand why his soldiers are treating the people with the patch of the yellow star on their clothes so badly and what was putting them on animal trains going to achieve? Or why parts of our city and Berlin are in ruins? Why do I never get see Edward and Gustav? Or why are we flying our planes over London for no reason? Why does the soldier in the black uniform want to find Abigail when I know he doesn't like her even though she hasn't done anything to him or anybody?

The Fuhrer made a great speech that everybody seemed to love but he didn't explain anything of what I wanted answered or he didn't mention anything about all the strange things that were happening in Germany or how things weren't really getting any better even though his speech made it sound as if they were getting better and everything was great.

Chapter Ten

The planes Sirens Flashing lights and Rumbling Sounds

We spent so much time waiting for the Fuhrer and then listening to his great speech that when we came back outside the sportpalast it was evening time. The snow was falling again and it was freezing cold and so dark that you could hardly see where you were going. There was no sign of any trams now and most of the crowd was walking with their heads down back into the city. Grandmother, Abigail and I weren't sure exactly where we were going now so we just followed the crowd back along the street where ever they were going in hope that we might see something we recognised. Not long after we came back into the part of the city where most of the buildings had been chopped in half. We were so cold and so worried now that the Fuhrer's great speech was now starting to become a distant memory and was almost forgotten. Grandmother held both our hands now and her hands felt so warm. It was the only part of me that felt warm as we walked through the city not sure which direction to take or which street to walk down.

Everything looked so much different at night time than it did earlier today when we were travelling on the tram. We walked for about an hour through the part of the city that was in ruins before we got back to what looked normal again. I had no idea what time it was now as I hadn't set Father's watch now since yesterday and it had stopped working. We stood into an arch way between two buildings now for shelter and tried to figure out where we were. The crowds were mostly gone now because unlike us they had found their way home. We didn't even know the name of the street that Grandmother lived on and I think there wasn't any point asking Grandmother as she probably couldn't remember it anyway.

I was really starting to get so worried now that I thought I should try to ask Grandmother in the hope that she might remember something.

'Do you think we will find our way home tonight?' Grandmother looked down at me and said.

'Sometimes you have to get lost first to find your way.' I looked at Abigail and we both shrugged our shoulders because we didn't know what grandmother was talking about. Grandmother was always coming out with one line sentences that really didn't make any sense at all. One of those lines she always loved to say was.

'It is never too late to be what you might have been.' Which I don't understand but can always remember it and another one she loves to say is.

'Do one thing every day that makes you happy.' Which I can understand and today being with Abigail and going to the sportspalast to see the Fuhrer has made me very happy.

Then it started and I stood there in shock. I could hear the sound of sirens that were almost deafening and the sound of planes in the sky. It was the first time I was ever outside at night time when the planes were flying over. Not long after we started hearing the planes in the sky the rumbling started in the distance. We could see the flashing lights not too far away after every rumble.

It reminded me of the thunder and lightning we would sometimes get during the summer months in the evenings, those evenings that were so warm that you could hardly breathe. But here tonight under this arch way it was freezing and the snow was falling even heavier now and it didn't look like it was going to stop.

During the summer we would count the seconds between the thunder and lightning to see how far away the storm was. One second for every mile but the rumbling tonight was followed straight away by the flashes coming from the ground and not like lightning that came from the sky.

We decided to stay under the arch way for safety and I bounced up and down on my toes to try to keep warm. The rumbling kept going for about the same amount of time as it took for about four inches of snow to build up on the footpath but thankfully the rumbling was always in the distance.

The breeze coming up the street once you stepped out was colder than I'd felt for a while and was as cold as the breeze on the bridge over the river in Dusseldorf. When the rumbling stopped and the sirens fell silent we started walking again and we arrived back to a part of the city that was busy and that we think we recognised. People had gathered on the streets and were standing around talking and pointing in the direction of where the rumbling and flashes of light had come from.

'More of the city has been destroyed by the bombing.' One man said.

'Hundreds of homes are gone and people are now homeless or worse.' I heard another man say.

'The sooner we get out of Berlin the better.' 'It's not safe anymore.'

'There'll be nothing left in this city by the time the war is over.'

I stood looking up at all the grownups talking and thought to myself how right they are.
We need to get out of not just Berlin but Dusseldorf too and thankfully we are all leaving on the first train in the morning.

'Do you have any idea where we are?' I asked Abigail.

'I think that's the street over there where we got on the tram this morning.' Abigail replied. And so it was.

'It looks so much different in the dark than it did this morning. We have to go straight down that street now and grandmother's house isn't much further away now.' We walked again so happy to be nearly home and after only about two minutes we turned a corner onto a narrow street and noticed that the street had been closed and it was being guarded by a group of soldiers. We tried walking in another direction down a different street hoping to bypass the soldiers to get home but all the streets had been closed and soldiers were everywhere stopping anybody who might be going back to that part of the city. Finally we approached the soldiers to ask them what was happening. As I looked around I noticed nobody else was out tonight on this street only grandmother, Abigail and I.

'Excuse me sir, my Grandmother lives on a street in that direction. I was just wondering can we get back home there tonight?' I was very nervous as I spoke to the soldiers and hoped that they wouldn't ask us our names Just in case one of them might know the soldier in the black uniform that was looking for Abigail back in Dusseldorf.

'Sorry but you won't be going back there for a while, there's nothing left in that direction. Most of it has been destroyed tonight by the bombing.'

'Are there any houses left and what about the people? My Mother was in Grandmother's house when we left this morning.' The soldier looked at me as if he were feeling sad but I'm not sure why. Then he just said.

'We're not sure what's going on and we won't know until morning when it gets bright and we can go in and see.' We looked in the direction of Grandmother's house and all we could see was a glowing of red from the fires that were burning. Surely Grandmother's house was gone now and was probably chopped in half like the houses we had seen this morning on the way to the sportpalast.

But where was Mother now and where would we find her at this time, in the dark in a city that we didn't know at all and in a city where we didn't know anybody either. All we knew at this stage was tomorrow morning we would be catching a train back home to see Father and Hans. Grandmother was coming too but she hadn't packed her case and we hadn't got anything with us either. I thought to myself maybe Mother has packed everything for everybody and was gone to the station to meet up with us now that Grandmother's old house was gone.

We walked back down the street away from the soldiers and stood and waited while we tried to figure out what to do. Grandmother had no idea what was happening and had already forgotten what the soldier had said and that her house was most likely gone.

'I think we should go back to the train station to see if Mother is there.'

'I think that would be the best idea and at least there we would get shelter from the snow and wind.' Abigail said. I could see that Abigail like I was shivering from the freezing cold. The snow hadn't stopped now since we had left the sportpalast and the last time I had felt warm was when we were inside listening to The Fuhrer making his speech. I'd say that the Fuhrer is somewhere warm now in a hotel or in his house planning on what he will do next to make everything great again.

I turned and walked back towards the soldiers to ask them how we would get to the train station as I couldn't remember how we had gotten here yesterday. At the time I wasn't really concentrating on what streets we were on but rather just admiring the buildings, flags and other trams on the streets and the people walking up and down. After I had asked the soldiers for directions to the station, one of them took out a piece of paper and wrote something on it. He folded it a few times and told me to give it to one of the soldiers at the station. He told me how to get there and that I wasn't to open the piece of paper under any circumstances. Now I'm sure what he meant by the word circumstances but I'm sure he meant for me not to open it no matter what happened.

That was another one of those words that only grownups used and I suppose now I could say, one of those words that only the Fuhrer might use in one of his great speeches about how he was making our country great again, one of his great speeches that everyone loved but didn't really answer any of the questions that I wanted answered. We headed back now walking as fast as we could to get to the station before we would get any colder if that was even possible. Grandmother was singing a song as we walked and she seemed to be so happy and not in the least bit worried about her house or finding Mother at the station or maybe not meeting up with Mother again till we get back to Dusseldorf.

The trams were back working again now and we jumped on one to bring us to the station. Grandmother was telling everybody on the tram how horses used to pull the trams and how it was much better back then. Everybody was smiling at her as she talked about the trams and the horses and then once again she started singing. Grandmother probably can't remember being at the sportpalast but when it came to singing an old song Grandmother could remember every word like she had written the song herself.

She started singing at the top of her voice the words. 'Du, du liegst mir am Herzen. du, du liegst mir am sinn. Du du machst mir viel Schmerzen.' And everybody on the tram joined in and sang the song with Grandmother. And for the next few minutes as we moved slowly through the streets of Berlin on that tram the crowd sang along to the rhythm of the tram which worked perfectly with the rhythm of the song as if they were made for each other. Even the people on the street that night smiled at the tram as it passed by. We arrived at the station and as we stepped off the tram everybody stood up and clapped and cheered for Grandmother. As the tram pulled away Grandmother turned and took a bow and then blew kisses at the people on board. Everybody smiled and clapped even more and cheered even louder as the tram drove away down the street and out of sight.

I thought for a moment while I stood watching Grandmother taking a bow and blowing kisses at the tram that she had lived all her life in Berlin and the house that she grew up in was now gone and tonight she was leaving and for one last time she was singing for the people of Berlin and taking a final bow. And thankfully for Grandmother she didn't even know what was happening and I'm just glad that she is so happy.

We went back inside the station and looked around us to see that the platforms were empty and there wasn't a train in sight. The ticket office was closed and it was dark and freezing cold. The breeze was blowing up the tracks and coming through the station which looked like it had been abandoned and was no place to be at this time of night.

Just then a soldier dressed in a black uniform like the soldier that was looking for Abigail appeared out from behind a door and asked us what we were doing there this late at night. I handed him the piece of paper the soldier had given me back near Grandmother's house and he opened it and looked at it for a couple of seconds.

'Come in here.' He said. 'You can stay the night here in the office and I will get the three of you onto the train back to Dusseldorf tomorrow morning.' He brought us into a beautiful warm office with a large fireplace and fire in it that was burning brightly. It looked a bit like Fathers book shop with timber floors and shelves covered in books. Only difference in here was it didn't look like it had a secret door but this office did have four long soft chairs for us to sleep on. We each picked a chair to sleep on for the night and the soldier put coats over us to help keep us warm.

'Get a good sleep tonight.' He said. 'And I'll wake you in the morning before the train has to leave. Don't worry about the fire I'll keep it burning for the night.'

I lay on the chair and smiled over at Abigail who was peeking back at me from under a large soldier's coat that had a small red and white flag wrapped around one of the sleeves. She smiled back at me and then without warning Grandmother started to snore. We both laughed as the soldier said. 'I thought I could hear the planes flying over again.'

This was the warmest I had felt for a long time maybe even since the winter had started. I thought to myself that Mother wasn't here at the station but hopefully she will arrive in the morning or we will meet back home in Dusseldorf tomorrow sometime. The room was glowing red from the fire and Abigail was asleep now too. I was struggling to get to sleep because it felt as if a horse was racing in my head with all the thoughts going through it from everything that had happened over the past twelve hours and over the past four of five days.

The soldier was humming a song that I thought I recognised and that I think I had heard somewhere before. I lay back trying to figure out what it was and wondering would I ask him the name of the song.

'Falling in love again (Can't help it).' The soldier whispered. I looked up at him a little confused and said excuse me? As I didn't know what he was saying or talking about. He looked at me and smiled and said.

'Falling in love again (Can't help it).' That's what that song is called and I heard it in a movie once but can't remember what the movie was called or what the girl's name was that sang it in the movie but it was beautiful.'

Falling in love again (Can't help it). What a great name for a song I thought.

The soldier kept humming and from time to time he would throw in a few words that he knew and then just hum for a while and then sing a full verse and then hum for a while as Grandmother snored and I looked at the ceiling and over at Abigail and closed my eyes and the humming seemed to fade and get further away.

Chapter Eleven

January 31th 1942
Day Six

Grandmother stays in Berlin

I woke the next morning with the soldier standing over me shaking me and whispering.

'Good morning. Wake up it's time to get up.'

I sat up and looked around trying to remember where I was as I always do when I wake up in a strange place. I looked across at Abigail who was still asleep and at Grandmother who had stopped snoring but was still asleep too. The fire had gone out during the night but the room was still really warm. The station outside was already busy with people getting ready to travel on trains to the countryside and some like ourselves were probably going back to Dusseldorf.

'Your train will be leaving shortly and I have gotten you three tickets already this morning.' The soldier said. 'You can wait in here till the train arrives as it's much warmer than out on the platform.' I stood up and walked towards the little window in the room beside the door that looked out at the station. There was a train on the platform that was already full and ready to pull out of the station. The soldier was now standing beside me and was leaning over and looking out through the window with me.

'That train is full with mostly children who are being evacuated out of the city to safety.' He said.

'The next train will be here in about five minutes and is for Jews who are being moved to a camp in Poland, it could be Auschwitz.' He said.

'And then your train will be along after that.' Now I understood what he meant by evacuated because I had heard Mother use the word when she had told us about going to the countryside but I didn't exactly know what he was talking about when he said Auschwitz or camps in Poland. All I knew was that Poland was a whole other country that I had heard about before and that The Fuhrer had mentioned it in his speech yesterday. And I didn't have a clue what he was talking about when he said Jews. I stood there with him right beside me and I was just too afraid to ask. He sounded like he really didn't like these Jews and was glad that they were leaving Berlin to go to the camp in Poland. I sat back down in my chair and thought to myself that I'll wait and get back up again when the next train arrives and I can see for myself who these Jews are and what these Jews look like. Not long after the train full with children going to the countryside pulled out of the station another one pulled in. 'I have to go now to help the rest of the soldiers with the Jews and to make sure everyone boards the train.' The soldier said, but by the tone of his voice he wasn't sounding too happy about having to leave his nice warm office and sounding as if these Jews were a nuisance to him. He left and closed the door after him causing a freezing cold breeze to blow through the room and wake Abigail. Abigail sat up and said.

'Good morning!' She looked like she was in a good mood this morning but I'm guessing it was mostly to do with the fact that she had a good night's sleep and this was probably the first time for a while she felt warm first thing in the morning.

We talked for a few minutes as quietly as we could so as not to wake Grandmother and then out of nowhere the commotion started out on the platform. We both ran to the window to see what was going on outside.

I was shocked and amazed all at the same time to see and to realise that the Jews the soldier was talking about were actually normal people who wore those yellow stars on their clothes just as Abigail and her parents did. Hundreds were being marched up the platform followed closely by a number of soldiers. Once again as we had seen at the freight station in Dusseldorf these people didn't seem too happy about having to be here. Nobody was talking or smiling but rather everyone had their heads facing the ground as they walked. Only one soldier this time had one of those large brown and black dogs and he could be heard louder than anything else in the station with the exception of course of the train. Everybody was crowding onto the train now as fast as they could and when you looked through the train window you could see some were lucky enough to have seats but most had to stand. Thankfully this time at least they had a proper train to travel on and not one of the animal trains like back in Dusseldorf. And thankfully this time also nobody got shot or hit by any of the soldiers while boarding the train.

'They must be going to the countryside today.' Abigail said.

'Yes I'm sure they must be and they have a nice train to go on too.'

We stood looking out the little window for the next at least twenty minutes watching what everybody was doing. I thought about why did the soldier call them Jews and why did he seem not to like them very much? It's all very strange that nobody likes the people with the yellow stars that I am now guessing are called Jews for some reason. If they are anything like Abigail you couldn't help but like them or even love them.

When the train was full it too pulled out of the station and the soldier came back into the office looking very happy to be back in a nice warm room. He went to the fire place and started cleaning out ashes and getting the fire ready to be lit again all the time mumbling to us about the cold out on the platform. I was hoping he wouldn't mention the word or use the word Jews or say anything about camps in Poland in front of Abigail. Now I wasn't even sure what camps were but I think the word countryside sounds a lot better.

I decided to bring up a subject that might distract him a little and make him forget about saying something bad in front of Abigail about the Jews or the camps so I asked him. 'That beautiful song you sang last night can you remember where you heard it?' 'Ah yes I can, it was in a movie called. 'Der Blaue Engel' and it was sung by the most beautiful girl I have ever seen but I can't remember her name. I can never remember the names of the actors or singers in the movies.'

And once again he started singing the words and humming the parts he didn't know. Grandmother had woken up and we didn't even notice until we heard her join in and sing the song with the soldier. She had a big smile on her face as she sang and the soldier smiled back at her now as he danced around the room waving his hands in the air and singing the new words he was learning from Grandmother.

When they both ran out of words to sing they just hummed at the top of their voices as Grandmother swayed from side to side in her chair and the soldier danced with his hands waving in the air. Abigail and I just laughed at them as we did last night on the tram. Grandmother always seemed to be happy but she was especially happy when she was singing and it always gave us a good laugh or just made us feel happy too. Grandmother just didn't seem to care what anybody thought of her or she never seemed to be shy or embarrassed by anything she did and everyone loved her for whatever she did.

While they were both still humming the song Grandmother put her head back in her chair and fell asleep again but only this time with a big smile on her face and she wasn't snoring. The soldier hadn't noticed and asked her did she know the name of the girl that sang the song. He danced and hummed and asked her a second time did she know who sang the song. Abigail and I were still laughing and Grandmother was still smiling and still asleep. The soldier stopped dancing and looked at

Grandmother sitting back on her chair. He looked a little confused as he approached her to see would she wake up again. He said nothing but just held his ear in front of her mouth and put his hand on the side of her neck for a couple of seconds and then on her wrist. I thought maybe he wanted Grandmother to whisper to him who was it that sang the song in the movie. He stood back up and turned to us and said.

'Your Grandmother is sleeping again. She must be just so tired god bless her.'

The soldier now had stopped singing and was sitting at his large office desk writing something on a large piece of paper while Abigail and I sat wrapped in soldier's coats while Grandmother slept. We waited for the train to arrive out on the platform but didn't mind too much that it was late as we were so comfortable and warm in here in the office and I wasn't really looking forward to going out into the cold and boarding the train for our long journey back to Dusseldorf.

The soldier finished writing his letter, folded it and put it into an envelope, sealed it and handed it to me and asked me to give it to my Father. I looked at the envelope and admired how nice it was. It had a stamp in one corner with a picture of The Fuhrer on it. I hadn't noticed the soldier put in on so I'm guessing the stamp must have been there already. I didn't have any bags so I put the letter in my pocket and said to Abigail that Hans collected stamps and that he would be delighted with this stamp with The Fuhrer on it. Just then the train pulled into the station. The soldier stood up and said. 'I will help you two onto the train and make sure you get seats. I have put it in the letter for your Father to read, that I think your

Grandmother is too tired to travel on the train today and that she might be better off waiting here at the station for your Mother to arrive. Another few hours sleep in the station and she might feel better rested and she can take the next train to Dusseldorf with your Mother.'

That was a great idea I thought as it was so cold out at the moment and Abigail and I would easily find our way from the station in Dusseldorf back home to our little shop on Bilker Street. We left the office and whispered goodbye to grandmother so as not to wake her. The soldier got onto the train with us and found us two seats side by side and facing in the direction we were going which I knew was better because Mother had said it was better and you wouldn't feel sick while travelling. We said goodbye to the soldier and he left just before the train pulled slowly out of the station and back on its long journey to Dusseldorf. I think he was probably the nicest soldier I had met in a long time and was more like Edward and Gustav, but the only thing was like most soldiers he didn't seem to like the people with yellow stars on their coats, and for some reason and for the first time I had heard it before he called them Jews.

I couldn't wait to get home and tell Father and Hans everything that had happened with Grandmother's house and how she was waiting back at the station for Mother to arrive and that we weren't sure where mother had gone. I couldn't wait to tell him about The Fuhrer and the sportpalast with the balconies up near the ceiling. I thought to myself that I must tell him about everything before I gave him the letter that the nice soldier had given me because then if he read that there would be nothing left to tell. I put my hand in my pocket to take the letter out when I noticed it wasn't there anymore.

'Oh no it's gone!' I said to Abigail.

'What's gone?' Abigail replied.

'The letter the soldier gave me for Father.' I said.
'But I think it should be fine as we can both tell Father everything that happened. The only thing is I won't be able to give Hans his stamp with the picture of the Fuhrer on it. He won't be too happy about that.'

'Don't tell him or even mention the letter and then nobody will be disappointed.' Abigail said.

'Yes brilliant idea Abigail.'

Abigail was always very clever like that and even though I only knew her for a few days I think she could always think of a solution to every problem. I sat back and relaxed and looked forward to getting home and going to the countryside afterwards. In my head I hummed the song that grandmother and the soldier were singing and I smiled to myself when I thought of Grandmother singing on the tram and when she got off the tram, the way she took a bow.

Chapter Twelve
Going back to Dusseldorf

The train journey back to Dusseldorf was going to take around five hours. Well at least that's what I think I can remember Mother saying when we were on our way here. Sometimes if something somebody says doesn't seem very important at the time, you don't really listen but now I wish I had because I'm not really sure now how long it's going to take. If I was told last week that I'd be travelling on a train with Abigail Blaustein for five hours, just the two of us, I'd have told you that you were mad because just a week ago I had never even spoken to Abigail Blaustein.

We had only been on the train for about an hour when the train slowed down and then after about one or two minutes of going really slowly the train stopped with the sound of screeching brakes. It was obvious that something was wrong as there was no reason for the train to stop here in the middle of nowhere. I looked out both sides of the train and could see nothing, no station, houses, buildings or even any people who might want to get on. Everybody now was up out of their seats looking out trying to figure out what was happening or why we had stopped. One man had his head sticking out through a narrow open window near the ceiling of the train. His head could hardly fit out and I don't even know how he managed it or if he would be able to get his head back in again. Or if the train started moving and he gets stuck out there, his head will surely have fallen off with the cold by the time we get back to Dusseldorf I thought to myself. Everybody had started to gather around him asking questions as he stood up on his seat with his backside facing the crowd.

'What do you see?'
'What's going on out there?'
'Why have we stopped?'
'Is there something blocking the tracks?'

Those were just a few of the questions being thrown at this faceless man who's trousers was now beginning to fall down just a little because he wore no belt or braces to hold them up and just enough now for everyone to see the top part of his backside. One man standing beside Abigail whispered to the lady beside him that the man's backside looked like the top of a money box and the little slit was where you had to put the money in. Some of the crowd that had gathered had now started to look away and others were smiling at each other. Abigail and I looked at each other and smiled and then looked back just as the man started to shout.

'I can see another train on the tracks in front of ours and I think I can see what looks like a second train in front of that one too.'

'Are you sure?' One lady asked.

'Why would there be three trains stopped one after another in the middle of nowhere?' Another said while trying not to look at the man with his head out the window and his backside up in the air facing the interested onlookers. The man then wiggled his backside from side to side while shouting.

'I'm not really sure why but it seems as if all the trains that left Berlin this morning are now stopped and waiting because I think something must be blocking the tracks.'

Everybody mumbled and whispered amongst themselves for a couple of minutes while the man with his head out the window was now turned around and facing everybody. He had a big red face and his chin and lips were blue and shaking from the cold. Everybody was now wondering and worrying about what was going to happen next or how long were we going to be stuck here. Just then two soldiers came onto our carriage from the front of the train and told everyone that the tracks had been damaged the night before during the air raid.

'How long are we going to be stuck here?'

'Not long sir. I'd say we should be pulling out of here very soon now. They have already started fixing the tracks and if anybody wants to get off the train and go for a walk they can do so, but nobody is to wander too far from the train just in case they miss us when we're leaving.'

'Will we get off and see what it looks like here in the countryside?' Abigail asked.

'What a great idea. It's not the countryside we'll be going to but at least we can get an idea of what it will be like.' I looked out at the heavy snow that was blowing in every direction and thought it's going to be freezing out there but we should be able to stick it for a few minutes. We went to the door and climbed down the two steps of the train and then had to jump the rest of the way to the ground. I landed in freezing snow that went straight up to my knees. Abigail jumped and landed beside me. This was deeper snow than I had ever seen before. It had just piled up really high on either side of the train tracks but when you went away from the tracks it wasn't as high. You would never have snow this deep in the city. The tracks were up high and ran along what seemed like the top of a hill with a large slope on either side of the train with about a twenty foot fall and going down at about a sixty degree angle. I knew this as we had just recently been talking about angles in school and I knew what a sixty, forty five and a thirty degree angle looked like but after that I wouldn't be sure what other angles looked like. I looked left and right and could see on my left that the people on the trains in front of us were sliding down the slope to the bottom and walking back up again. We walked in their direction to get a closer look. With every step I had to lift my foot at least up to my knee to get through the snow.

When we got closer I could see that everyone was sliding down the slope on their coats or some had emptied their suit cases and were sitting in one side of an open suit case with their feet on the other side. Most of the coats being used were coats with the yellow star on them just like Abigail used to have but left behind at the freight station. People were screaming as they went down the slope and laughing when they got to the bottom. One suit case had a child in either section, one behind the other and they both laughed and held their hands in the air as they slid to the bottom.

When I looked back towards our train they had all started to do the same. I had never heard such laughing and screaming and

133

so much fun in my life before. I now knew that everybody going to the countryside was a brilliant idea. The children of Berlin and Dusseldorf, the families that wore the yellow star on their clothes and anybody else that was going were far better off in the countryside. I just couldn't wait to go.

I took off my coat and lay it on the ground. I put the collar facing towards the bottom of the slope and sat down on it. I put my feet in the holes for the sleeves and pulled the sleeves back towards me and held them tightly like the rains of a horse. Abigail gave me a push on the back and swooosh.

I flew faster than I have ever done before like a bird diving to catch a fish floating near the top of the river. My heart was racing with excitement and a little bit of nerves thrown in too. This was the best thing I'd done for as long as I could remember. I climbed out and back to the top of the hill. Abigail sat down, held the rains and I gave her a push and off she slid screaming all the way to the bottom.

We took turns now going down the slope and as I looked around I could see hundreds of people were now sliding. Men and women with the yellow star on their clothes, and the ones who didn't have a yellow star like Abigail and I. Soldiers and children from the front of the first train which was full with children to the back of our train, people were laughing and screaming in the heavy snow. Soldiers were carrying children on their backs back to the top of the slope and helping them back into their suit case and giving them a good push back to the bottom. For the first time while outside this winter I didn't feel in the least bit cold and I don't think I have ever had so much fun, or have I seen so many people having such fun together and I have never seen time go by so fast. I don't think I will ever forget the sight of over a thousand people from three different trains all playing together in the snow.

One man threw a snowball at another. He turned and said.

'I don't want to get into a snowball fight with you.' But then bent down and picked up a snowball and threw it back at him. That's the thing with a snowball fight, you are never happy when you get hit by a snowball and you never want to join in but you just can't for some reason resist throwing one back and then before you know it you're in a snowball fight. I looked around and everybody had joined in on the fight. The soldiers too were even throwing snowballs at each other.

It was starting to get dark when the soldiers who were watching the work that was being done at the front of the train now started to walk the length of the three trains telling everyone to get back on board. Abigail and I said good bye to the children we had met with the yellow stars while sliding and said that we hoped we would meet again when we all arrived at the countryside. We promised them we would look out for them when we got there next week.

While we were climbing back on the train I noticed that one couple and their two children that were on the train in front of ours were now climbing back onto our train. They had left their coats behind, maybe at the bottom of the slopes buried under the snow because when I looked around I couldn't see anything left behind. They had their suitcases with them and climbed on board like they were supposed to be there and nobody paid any attention to them what so ever. I decided to say nothing because it wasn't really any of my business and Mother always said that everyone should always mind their own business and nobody else's. I felt I should tell them that the train they were on before was a lot nicer than the trains from Dusseldorf to the countryside for people with the yellow star on their clothes. But I suppose now that they had gotten rid of their coats like Abigail had done at the freight station that maybe now they might travel on a nicer train from now on.

Back on the train now it felt really warm and I hung my coat on the back of the seat in the hope that it might dry before we got back to Dusseldorf. I sat by the window and Abigail sat as close as she could beside me. Abigail said her hands were freezing so I told her I would try to keep them warm for her. I held her hands up to my mouth and tried to breathe warm air on them. The train started to move ever so slowly again and Abigail and I sat back and held hands as Abigail rested her head on my shoulder and fell asleep.

The train was now about another hour into its journey and the snow had stopped outside. I could see that there was another full moon tonight and it was so bright outside it looked as if it could be the middle of the day. I sat looking out as we moved through the countryside and tried to remember the song the soldier had been singing or even the song that Grandmother had been singing on the tram but they were both gone. I couldn't remember their names or any of the words in them. I thought I will have to get Grandmother to teach them to me when Mother and her arrive back to Dusseldorf. I wondered where Mother must be tonight. I wondered if Mother and Grandmother had finally met and were they both sitting nice and warm in the soldier's office at the station singing songs along with the soldier.

It was now the middle of the night and it was probably going to be morning before we got back to Dusseldorf. Back to Father and Hans and back home to our little shop on Bilker Street which I now had decided was my favourite street in the world. I looked around the carriage and everyone was asleep now, even the man that had his head stuck out the window and his backside facing the crowd and telling us what was happening outside. Everyone was asleep and I felt as if I was the only one in the world that could see how beautiful everything looked with the full moon shining down on the blanket of snow that covered Germany tonight.

I wondered if the people on the train in front of us that we had played with on the slopes were asleep or could they see how beautiful everything looked.

I thought how lucky they were that they were already on their way to the countryside and would probably be there tomorrow playing and having fun in the snow and sliding down the slopes.

I tried again to remember the songs that the soldier had sang and that Grandmother had sang on the tram but they just wouldn't come back to me. My eyes were feeling tired now so I put my head back and closed my eyes and tried to sleep but I couldn't. I was tired enough and my eyes were sore but my thoughts just wouldn't let me go to sleep.

Chapter Thirteen

February 1st 1942
Day Seven
The blood on the floor and the Secret Door

I woke to hear the screeching of brakes and a loud whistling sound followed by the hissing of the steam rising and people shouting. I opened my eyes to see we had arrived back at Dusseldorf train station and the platform was full with people waiting to board our train. Everyone was starting to wake now and look around them with more than confused looks on their faces. It only seemed like five minutes ago we were sliding on the slopes but now here we were and it was time to go. The train must have travelled all night. I wasn't sure what time it was now as I hadn't set Fathers pocket watch since we were in Grandmothers house the night she had gotten the cobble stone from Hans. Which reminded me I was going to let him know as soon as we got home that I didn't think it was very funny that I had to carry it all the way to Berlin. I didn't think it was very funny at all even if everyone else did. But I knew I was wasting my time because he was only going to have an even better laugh at me. Maybe I would be better not to mention it at all.

Abigail and I stood up and walked down the aisle of the train towards the door. We got down off the train and onto a very busy platform. The crowds were waiting for us to get off and as soon as the door was clear they started to jump on board. We walked down the platform towards the front door of the station and out onto the street.

I turned and looked back at the clock tower to see the time. It was seven forty five in the morning and I wound Fathers watch and set it to the right time. Abigail and I walked back up the street towards home still holding hands and I was just feeling so happy to be back in Dusseldorf and so happy to be so close to home. The sun was shining and it was feeling a little bit warm but I still looked forward to getting back to the nice cosy warm shop.

I was feeling really hungry now too as I hadn't had anything to eat since yesterday morning in the office of the train station in Berlin. I was looking forward now also to getting something to eat and Abigail was probably feeling the same.

We arrived back into the town square the one with the statue of the horse with the man on his back with the long hair and silly hat and The Town Hall behind it. Nothing had changed since we had left and everywhere was still, as always covered in snow and the buildings covered with the red flags. I couldn't wait to tell Father about The Fuhrer and singing on the tram and how so many houses in Berlin were knocked down or chopped in half. I couldn't wait to tell him how Grandmother's house was knocked down too and that we weren't sure where Mother was but Grandmother was waiting for her at the station and they both will probably arrive home tomorrow. We arrived back on Bilker Street and as we walked back towards home I remembered the mean soldier in the black uniform that was looking for Abigail. I looked at Abigail and she still looked like she could be a boy. I hoped he had given up looking for her at this stage and that he wouldn't arrive back at the shop again with his large brown and black dogs.

We got to the front door and when I pushed it open the bell rang and when I closed the door behind me the bell rang again. We hadn't taken two steps across the shop floor when Father came running into the shop with an anxious look on his face. He said as fast as he could.

'Abigail quick, you'll have to hide. The soldiers have been here every morning since you've been to Berlin.' He grabbed Abigail by the arm and brought her to the secret door. Pushed the door open and Abigail rushed inside. He closed the door and said.

'Wait in there Abigail and stay as quite as possible especially if you hear anyone coming in through the front door.' Just then no sooner than Father had closed the secret door, the bell rang again. I turned and looked up at who had just come in? It was the soldier in the black uniform. I looked up at him and I noticed he had a serious look on his face but with a smile that looked like he had just gotten some great news or he had just been told a secret but nobody was ever going to find out. He looked down at me with his terrifying eyes and said.

'Where have you been the past few days?'

'I was in Berlin with Mother.'
I was shaking now with nerves as I wasn't really ready for this

and just wanted to get something to eat and tell Father about everything that had happened.

'You've been to Berlin with your Mother and where is she now?'

'I'm not really sure.' Father was standing back now looking a little surprised and I knew he must be confused also.

'You don't know where your Mother is?' He said sounding as if he knew more than I did.

'Well I'm not sure exactly, she could be with Grandmother at the station in Berlin and she might be home tomorrow.'

'Was your little brother with you in Berlin?' Father was standing behind me and the soldier standing over me looking down at me and I wasn't sure now how I should answer that question. I tried to remember what the plan was or had the soldier already seen Hans when he was here yesterday.

'Yes Hans was with us in Berlin.' I said hoping this was the right answer. 'And where is he now?'

'He's up stairs I think or maybe in the kitchen getting something to eat.'

'Was that him that just came in the front door with you a few minutes ago?' The soldier said looking down at me as if he hated me or I had done something really bad to him.

'Yes that was Hans. I think he will be back down in a few minutes.' I could hear Father turning and going towards the hall and out to the bottom of the stairs and shouting. 'Hans can you come downstairs at once.' I knew then that so far I had answered the questions just fine and when Hans comes downstairs it will look as if we have both just arrived back from Berlin and Abigail should be safe behind the secret door.

Han's came back down the stairs and into the shop and before he could say anything or before the soldier started asking anymore question's Father started asking his own questions not only to cover up for Hans or I making any mistakes but because he wanted to know what was happening.

'What has happened to Mother and Grandmother and why are you two boys arriving back from Berlin without them?' Everybody looked at me waiting for an answer and all with the same as usual confused looks on their faces including Han's who wasn't supposed to be confused because he was in Berlin with me. The soldier stood over me looking down with a sort of displeased look on his face. There was so much to tell that I didn't know where to start.

'Well. Where are they?' Father said again.

'I'm not really sure where Mother has gone because when we arrived back from the sportpalast to Grandmothers house it was gone and we stayed at the station and Grandmother waited there for Mother to arrive and we came home.' I said as fast as I could and without taking a breath.

'Slow down Deiter please and tell us what happened in Berlin and why you came back alone?'

'Grandmother brought us to the sportpalast to see The Fuhrer making his great speech and Mother didn't come.' The soldier was looking down at me now and I noticed a smile was coming across his face. I think the mention of the Fuhrer was making him happy.

'When we left the sportpalast to walk home we got a little lost and had to hide under an archway from the snow and while the planes were flying over. When we got back to Grandmother's street we were told by some soldiers that all the houses and buildings were gone. So we didn't know where Mother was, so we took a tram to the train station. We stayed at the station for the night with a very kind soldier in his office and the next morning we came home on the train and the soldier said that Grandmother should stay with him and wait for Mother to arrive.' Now everybody was silent and looking as if trying to figure it all out. The soldier now wasn't looking as serious as before and looked up at Father and said.

'I will contact Berlin and speak to the soldier at the station and try to find out what is happening. I will let you know what is happening as soon as I know.' Father thanked the soldier and the soldier turned to leave. He opened the door of the shop and before he could walk out another soldier walked in with a large brown and black dog with him. The dog had a lead around his neck and was pulling the soldier into the shop. Father didn't say anything about the dog inside on his shop floor as he had so much else to think of and he knew they were all about to leave.

'We have searched all the houses on this street.' The soldier said.

'Do you want me to search this house now?' We all looked up at the two soldiers in shock, my heart nearly stopped but only for a second as the soldier in the black uniform just replied. 'No not today, we'll come back tomorrow. Leave these good people in peace now.'

There was a sigh of relief from Father that must have been heard as the soldiers opened the door and the bell over the door rang. Just then the dog started to bark and jump up on his back legs as he tried to get away from the soldier and back into the shop. The soldier in the black uniform started shouting.

'CONTROL HIM. GET HIM OUT OF HERE NOW!'

The dog broke away from the soldier and ran back into the shop dragging his lead behind him, his lead that was actually a chain and it rattled as he ran across the floor and straight over to the secret door.

Father ran and grabbed his lead and tried to drag him away but the more he tried the more the dog fought and the more the dog barked. The soldier grabbed the lead and both of them were now pulling the dog as he barked and scratched and jumped towards the secret door. They now both managed to get the dog back towards the front shop window as the soldier in black slowly walked over to the secret door and now totally ignoring the barking dog, but only showing interest in the book shelves that the dog was barking at.

He walked up and down limping as he did very slowly in both directions from the front of the shop to the back and then back to the front again just looking at the shelves as he walked. He took his gun from the black holster on his right hip. He started tapping it on the shelves as he passed. Once more he walked slowly from the front to the back of the shop all the time tapping his gun on the shelves. He had a look on his face as if he were pleased or happy about something he had just achieved. He looked like a man that had just won something really important. The dog had stopped barking and everything now was silent. You could hear nothing only the sound of his footsteps and the tapping of his gun. Everybody waited and wondered what was going to happen next. Even the dog sat silent and looked with his head tilted to one side in anticipation.

Han's and I stood together near the door that led to the kitchen on one side of the shop and Father, the soldier and the dog stood over by the window. I was feeling sick and a little dizzy. I felt as if I was going to pass out. I thought to myself what was Abigail doing now on the other side of the book shelves. Was she peeking back through the shelves at us? Or was she taking the gun from the table drawer and putting bullets into it? Or was the gun even still in there? Or had she forgotten about it? Or was she hiding under the office table?

The soldier was still tapping on the shelves but now he had stopped walking and was standing right in front of where the secret door was. I think he noticed that on this section of shelves the books were packed tightly together so as not to fall off when opening the door. They also were the type of books that most people would never read. He put his hand on the shelf at around elbow height and started moving it around slowly. This is where the handle for opening the door was

145

hidden. There wasn't a sound as he moved his hand slowly around the shelf searching for what he knew was there and then he stopped as his hand found the groove in the timber that you could use to hold onto to

push open the door. As he started to open the secret door Father ran over and shouted.

'That's my office and you can't go in there!' The soldier turned to Father just as he got there and raised his gun and hit Father as hard as he could with the handle of his gun near the top of his head over his right eye and where his hair meets his forehead. Father dropped to the floor close to the book shelves and fell right in front of both Hans and I. And the blood poured out of his head as he lay there on the floor not moving or looking like he wasn't even breathing. Hans ran out of the shop and I could hear him running up the stairs. The blood flowed along the timber floor and under a gap at the bottom of the book shelves and into the office.

I was now on my knees on the ground and I don't even remember kneeling down. I could see the blood flowing under the shelves and into the office and I wondered if Abigail could see it too. The soldier opened the door and went inside. I could hear him walk in the direction of the office table which was just on the opposite side of the shelves to where Father was lying and to where I was kneeling. Then silence for a few seconds. All I could hear was the dog breathing.

'NEIN'! The soldier screamed. BANG! A gun shot.

Just one shot and a crashing sound as someone fell to the floor. Then blood flowed back out into the shop from the other side of the book shelves and along the floor board right beside the one that Father's blood was on. They were side by side on either floor board and were exactly the same colour. It was like they had come from the same person. The blood from both sides of the book shelves then flowed at the same time down between the floor boards into the gap and joined up and mixed together as they did.

Still there was complete silence as I watched this happen. Complete silence as I watched soldiers running in the front door and running around the shop with guns in their hands and the dog jumping around trying to get free and his mouth opening and closing and no sound coming out. While everything was so quite I started thinking about the time Abigail had kissed me just inside the secret door and how it made me so happy and it was the best day of my Life.

I was moving along the floor going backwards with somebody holding the collar of my coat. I could see Father getting further away and out of sight as I went around the corner of the book shelves passed the red chair and out the front door of the shop onto the street. I was left sitting on the street outside now and looking back in the front door of the shop as more soldiers ran in. I could see that Father's pocket watch had fallen out of my pocket and was on the ground just outside the front door but I just couldn't reach it. The street was filling up outside all around me with people looking at me and trying to look through the window of the shop and in the door trying to see what was going on. An old lady stood over me and was talking to me but I just couldn't hear her. Everything was silent and the old lady probably thought I wasn't very nice because I didn't answer her. She probably knew me or knew my Mother and Father and probably went to school with my Grandmother.

Hans, Abigail and Father were all still inside and nobody had come out yet. I sat looking at the ground afraid to look up and waited for them to come out. Then the first sound I heard was the sound of a car. It stopped close to me and someone got out and spoke to the soldiers. I looked up and could see the soldiers pointing at me so I looked back at the ground again. I was picked up by somebody and put into the back of the car and it drove away. I'd never been in a car before and as it drove along the bumpy cobble stones I was feeling sick. I lay down across the back seat of the car and closed my eyes and listened to the engine humming. It sounded a bit like the train or the tram only more of a continuous humming sound. With my eyes closed all I could see now was Abigail standing in front of me with a smile on her face and she was talking to me but I couldn't understand or hear what she was saying. She smiled at me once again and waved goodbye and faded away into the distance.

Chapter Fourteen

February 2nd 1942

Day eight

Waking up in the countryside

Standing here in this strange bedroom, in this strange place looking out through the small circle of clear glass on the frosted window that I made with the side of my fist I wondered where I was and how I had even gotten here. I wondered where Father and Mother were. Had Mother arrived back to Dusseldorf with Grandmother and found that I wasn't there anymore? Where had Hans and Abigail gone? Would they be coming to the countryside with Mother as soon as she got back from Berlin? I knew Father was to stay in Dusseldorf to look after the shop. I looked out through the window at this strange place with no houses or streets, no cars, trams or people, only a wire fence in the distance and for the first time in my life I felt alone. I have always liked to spend time on my own but I've never felt alone before. I look now around the room at all the beds in here with nobody sleeping in any of them. Rows of beds stacked one on top of the other just like the one I slept in last night and then the door opens and another boy walks in. I stand face to face with this strange boy, who is wearing even stranger clothes and with a coat that has a number on it that is too long for me to remember. He is exactly the same height as me only he is a lot thinner and he has no hair.

'Hello. I'm Peter what's your name?' He asks.

'Deiter.' I reply. 'Where am I, is this the countryside?'

'No this is a camp. Are you an orphan?'

'Yes.'

Somebody calls from outside and he leaves again. Now I don't know what he was talking about but I pretended I did and so I told him I was an orphan and I don't even know what that is. I didn't want to sound like I was silly in front of somebody that I have never met before.

I look back out the window and I could see tracks in the snow which looked like they were made by the wheels of a car, but they were fading as more snow falls. I wished that another car would come up the driveway to this strange place along those tracks and everyone I know would get out. I'm not even sure who else is in this strange place or who else could be outside the door. I can't hear anything only the sound of my own breathing and my body shaking now with the cold. I jump back into bed to try to remember my dream and maybe go back there and also to get warm again. I cover my head with these blankets that are not the same as the blankets at home or as soft but just hard and damp and cold. I lie in the dark and exhale outwards warm breaths of air to try to warm up under these cold blankets.

After a couple of breaths I feel a little dizzy, sick and mostly hungry.

I close my eyes and think to myself where could everybody be? I try to remember the song that Grandmother sang on the tram so I can sing it to myself to help me feel better, but like always I've forgotten the words, the air and everything about it. Only the look on Grandmothers face as she sang it and the look on everyone's faces as they joined in. I close my eyes even tighter and try to imagine I'm back there on the tram going to the station with Grandmother and Abigail. I can see Grandmother singing, I can see Abigail smiling at me. Hans and Father are sitting across from me now beside Grandmother. Abigail and Mother are sitting either side of me. Abigail looks really happy as she looks around at everyone on the tram singing and then looks back at me and smiles at me again. I can see everything but I can't hear anything.

Then slowly the sound is coming back and getting louder and louder and everyone is laughing and singing. I can see two soldiers walking in the distance towards us that look like Edward and Gustav and I can hear the sound of the tram, the rhythm of the tram and I can see the snow falling and feel the cold air. The song and the tram are moving at the same time, the same rhythm and the people on the street are smiling. An old man stands on the street in an old soldier's uniform smoking a pipe and he salutes as we pass by. Then I can hear the song and everyone singing it.

'Du, du liegst mir am Herzen. du, du liegst mir am sinn. Du du machst mir viel Schmerzen.'

This time I join in and when I look at Abigail she's singing it too. She looks happy, happier than she has looked since I first met her in the shop, happier than she has looked since I first seen her playing outside on Bilker Street. I feel warmer and I don't close my eyes as tightly now but I keep them closed and keep singing along. Abigail and I are singing now louder than anyone and we keep smiling at each other as we do.

'Du, du liegst mir am Herzen. du, du liegst mir am sinn. Du du machst mir viel Schmerzen.'

I lie here under the blankets and I can see everyone smiling which makes me feel happy. I feel the tears now coming from my eyes too because I know this is only a dream.

THE END

CPSIA information can be obtained
at www.ICGtesting.com
Printed in the USA
BVHW041539051222
653478BV00010B/59